The Decadent

Mary Elizabeth Brazil

ISBN: 9781505241815

DEDICATION

These pages are dedicated to the 'greats' who have influenced and expanded my mind

And for my Father

Who never quite left mine

1. Baltimore - 1849

I forgot most of my kills. It was a safety mechanism, protection from any guilt that I may possibly harbour. Imagine carrying the sins of centuries from terminating lives to enhance your own one. My mind had to block out the memories. It was difficult, though I had mastered how to control most of the unwanted data. Some kills came back to haunt me now, despite my best efforts, and some came back like long lost friends who I eagerly embraced. One particular Master came back as the latter.

As I sat back sipping my red wine, a poor substitute for the essence enhancing that I needed but a substitute nonetheless, I smiled to myself as I remembered my last day with him.

It was in Baltimore that I broke the rules; you see when I had taken the life force of creative people before I had ensured that they died before I left them. I always make it look like suicide, hence why it seems that so many artists and creative people kill themselves. They do not. I kill them.

I could not bring myself to kill the physical form of this one though. I had been observing him for so long that I had bonded with him. No, it was more than that for I had spied on other Masters for the same time duration as him. This is a time for honesty. If a story is to be told, let it be told from the heart. I think I was in love with him or as close to love as I was capable of. It felt strange to 'love' somebody who I had never met on a personal level, until that night, and yet 'love' him I had or at least I thought I had.

I knew how he would smell. I knew what tone the sound of his voice would carry, as I conversed with him, for I had observed him for so long from a safe distance. His every gesture was an echo from my years as his stalker. I was besotted for want of a better word.

I wondered in awe at him and the way that he broke down literary boundary after the next. When somebody as godly as him resided on the planet I saw it as a blasphemous act to 'snuff' out his life. Let me say though as I use the words 'godly' and 'blasphemous' that there is no God and I use the word in the descriptive sense and not in the verifying sense. I say that there is no God as I have never encountered 'Gods' over the centuries as I dance with death. Feel free to correct me if you feel that you have evidence that squash my thoughts on deities. Only correct me with evidence and not with the blind faith that causes me to suffer from nausea.

Let me continue in Baltimore and leave blind faith at the door. I could not take this Master's physical life, for reasons explained, and so after spending the night drinking with him and swapping stories of life and loves, I simply walked away. I had never done this with one of my kills before.

He told me stories of his love life which I could not partake in for I had never really known love in the way that he described. I told him stories of the centuries that I had lived through. He saw my narrative as a figment of my imagination and, being a writer, he greedily drank it down. How could he have known that my many lives narrative was true? It was, after all, when dissected in the objective sense by myself, so totally unbelievable.

How could my eyes have seen the ancient philosophers and yet my mouth be drinking with this genius in Baltimore in the 1800s?

How could I have lived in the early part of the 19th century and yet walk the streets of the present day, in your time? Time was not my master. I controlled time and I was undefeatable where the clocks were concerned.

We spoke of the calamities that invade the everyday being and then we grew tired. That moment came when conversation became exhausted. Silence and the odd sigh and sip of wine filled the air instead. There was no awkwardness that silence can bring with it. We relished the absence of conversation as much as we did its' presence. Our silence only made us communicate with each other more as we stared into one another's eyes and then around the room.

Did I want him sexually? I cannot say for sure. I felt I loved him but intercourse seemed too obvious, too coarse for us. Sex always makes a mockery out of love in the end. Once body fluids have been exchanged and carnal pleasures shared, love seems to become less sacred. The easiest thing to do in the world is to have sex. It is so much harder to love.

I decided that we should change clothes. I have no idea why I suggested this but I did. I guess it was because this man knew how to dress and I wanted to mimic his style and what better way than by wearing the shirt off the man's back?

We had laughed as we toppled over trying to remove trousers before our shoes. Little did the writer know that he was dressing for his death. Had he known of the fate to come he would have chosen a more stylish, flamboyant outfit. He certainly would not have exchanged clothes with me. Style was a stranger to me for the material world was not my friend. Material things change. They evolve and become strangers to us, relics of our past.

I lived for emotions, for the effects that the life force of creative people could give me. This man's life, like so many other individuals responsible for enhancing the lives of the human race, was as vibrant and self-destructive as a beautiful flower choosing to dance in a storm. I wanted to pluck that flower, to wear it on me, to smell it and then crush it in my hands.

Once our clothes were exchanged we sipped a little more wine before I executed the manoeuvre that I was so familiar with now. To the uninitiated eye it would seem as though I was stroking the neck of the writer. I was in fact 'pulling' from his body and through his skin the part that made him the genius that he was, his pineal gland.

I cannot recall the moment that I realised that I had to live on a diet of the pineal glands of the creative Masters throughout time. I just know that I have to. I have tried not to consume them and I have nearly died. That first time that I swallowed a gland though, like the first time that a human loses their virginity, should not be lost to my mind. It is though. I have spent many nights trying to recall the beginnings of the nature of my existence and I come up with nothing. Perhaps the memory is too terrible to capture. Perhaps one day it will come to me and I will know my true beginnings.

I always stare at the cone shaped uncalcified gland before consuming it like a tablet. Most humans have calcified pineal glands but in Masters the gland never calcifies. This is what makes them who they are. Calcification must stunt creativity and make you the regular mortals who you are. You dance with your nine to five jobs and allow others to fill your mind with wonder. You read the work of Masters on public transport or listen to their creative endeavours through your advanced music devices. They produce the wonder and shun normality and it is all down to a lack of calcification. I can think of no other explanation for why their minds are capable of such beauty.

I stare at the gland with an expression of guilt mixed with joy for it is not mine to take and yet I need it and want it so. There is little choice in the matter for me though you, of course, may argue this. No argument will change the facts though.

The writer felt faint and fell back in his chair. He thought it was the wine for what else could it be? How was he to know that the part of his body, the creative part, had been robbed from him and that he would never be capable of inspiration again? A cruel fate for an innovative writer I am sure you would agree? It is like severing the hands of a celebrated pianist or slashing the face of the most beautiful woman on earth.

I began the state of ecstasy that I always fell into following the stealing of the essence of a creative Master. I could not kill him though. Even as I watched the confused writer in my ecstatic state I knew that I could not take him. Without the mind this man was nothing. His body had just been a vessel carrying his genius around. Even though I knew that by taking his creative force I had effectively killed him, I did not need to see another dead body. There would be no more decomposing flesh tonight. Not here in Baltimore. I wanted my kill to walk away from me for once. He would walk and die elsewhere and not at my hands. It was the closest gesture to love I had ever acted out, at that point in my life. I had taken the writer's essence from him and abandoned him to his fate. Even the ones who I 'loved' I treated appallingly. I deserved loneliness.

How many dead bodies had I seen over the centuries as who I found myself to be? No abacus could count it then; no master computer could calculate the sum now. So many Masters consumed by my want and needs. Their essences were embedded in my bones, woven into my veins. Their work kept my heart beating, kept the blood pumping around my alien body.

When the writer found his feet, he stumbled while murmuring my false name that I had called myself. I was no longer there though and even if I had been the writer would not have remembered his time with me. All he remembered was a name and he called it out on the streets of Baltimore as the pavement ate at his feet.

He called the name as he collapsed into the arms of passing strangers and how roughly they caught him for they knew not who he was. They would have caught him gently had they known that the man who lay before them would never rise again.

History would record his death in a poor fashion. They

never recorded the fates correctly. How could they when they are not in possession of the facts? Ambiguity reigned supreme in the deaths of creative Masters who flood the lands of time. Some paint, some write, some act, some create music that lifts you to the levels of 'angels' and me? I just fed, I fed on them all from country to country and century to century, not knowing why I had to but doing it all the same.

2. London - present day

I said earlier that I do not know love. I have read about love and have studied the great works of poetry and plays regarding the matter. I have observed paintings and sculptures that try to define the impossible subject that is love. I have 'known' women and men. Drunken, stolen moments of lust and witnessed their traces of crippling regret after the act. I had kissed the dying lips of some of my kills with a feeling close to love but not love for love is something that we should recognise when it happens apparently. I have never experienced this recognition. My mind does not know and understand love in its' natural form. It replicates, I fornicate but unlike time, I cannot conquer love. I am not sure if this causes me dismay or not. I have lived centuries without it though. I do not need love in the same way that I need my essence enhancing.

My present Master fixation is making me question love again. I am in London. The economic climate is not inviting or the heat wave that is normally a stranger to the streets. While I am not human, my body appears to feel temperature changes in the same way that your biological makeup does. I do not know how the weather can conduct the body of something like me but it can. Perhaps I am half human? I digress. I love this London because the soon to be Master, Roberta Downs, lives here.

Before I discuss Roberta Downs I need to tell you a bit about her history. Willow Downs, mother of Roberta, was a famous author whose book, 'Timelines for lines' must be on every bookshelf in the world. Written in the 1970's when she was twenty five, it has become I guess what you would call a 'cult classic'. Willow Downs was a 'victim' of mine.

I shall set the scene for you. It is London and the year is 1977. London hosted the Eurovision contest, Sweden won Miss World, there were neo-Nazi demonstrations in South London and I took the life force of Willow Downs. Sometimes I can still hear her husband calling for her, unaware that I had killed her.

I had taken Willow's pineal gland and I had slit her wrists to make it look like suicide. It was messier than I had hoped it would be. I was expecting blood of course but she really bled which disappointed me slightly as it tainted our time together. I can remember feeling annoyed about it as I watched the blood covering her lifeless veins. I had needed that essence though and so a little inconvenience had to be endured.

I do not like recalling this to you all of a sudden. I cannot say I feel guilty about leaving Willow's husband, Clarke, to clean up my mess. I just wish there had not been so much blood spilled in the first place. She would not stay still though so Willow had to take part of the blame for the distressing scene that awaited her unsuspecting husband.

I am standing near the window and I have chosen not to be seen. I have the ability to do this though I do not know how. Once again, it is one of the many mysteries surrounding my existence that cannot be explained at this moment in time. I can simply disappear before your eyes if necessary and sometimes it has been very necessary.

I should hate myself for loitering to see Clarke's reaction more than the action of taking the gland but I cannot help myself. I want to witness his pain. I know that it will add to the rush of Willow's essence and it is all about my pleasure. I want to be delayed from coming down from the effects of her gland and Clarke's grief can help me do this. I am a detestable creature when I think about it. I shall not think about it.

Clarke's eyes witness what no loving husband should

have to. He sees the blood dripping from his dead wife that has turned the bathwater a milky red. Willow's eyes are open with a look of horror on them. She is staring straight at Clarke, her head tilted on the side. There is no love there for Clarke to seek solace in. No peace. He looks down and sees that the snow white carpet is dotted with his wife's life force. I notice that Clarke stifles a scream and the need to be sick. A hand reaches for his and it can only be his daughter, Roberta. I thought that she was asleep. Not that her being awake would have changed my course of action. I did not want to see the child suffer though. I am not a complete monster.

Now husband and daughter are both witnessing what they should not. They are the audience to the suicide of their wife/mother. Life changes after that for the worse I would imagine for you mortals. All you have is your life really. I do not need to be human to know that. They cannot come back from it. I have seen enough of my damage and leave them to the ruins of their lives. I owe them nothing so forgive me for my lack of compassion regarding the matter. No, that is not the right thing to say. I must try to be honest. I must try to write the truth in case this account is found one day. I have a little compassion for them but not enough to dwell on it or regret it.

Now in present day London, Willow's daughter, Roberta Downs, is an aspiring author and I am back in her life. Does she want to write because of her mother's chosen career? Does she feel that the only way to get close to her dead mother is to make her writing come alive? I do not have the answers but what I can tell you is ten thousand words into her latest attempt at a novel, this is her masterpiece. Her debut novel is the one. I know it. I feel it just like I have felt all of the masterpieces before hers. The feeling is not as intense as it has been in past decades but it is definitely there.

How do I have this gift? This remains unanswered too. How disappointing if you are the kind of person who needs answers. I have so few for you at present. Perhaps as my words unfold I will discover things about myself and you will discover them with me. I do not know how I am what I am and yet here I sit opposite her in this cafe.

I have been watching her since she was a baby for I had been watching her mother. I had watched Roberta grow within her mother's womb though I had not sensed at the time that she would have Master potential. I was too distracted by her mother's genius to notice Roberta's gift at the time.

I felt strange about Roberta. It was hard to explain. I wanted her pineal gland but I wanted her more at times it would seem. Was it wrong, after killing her mother, to want her also? I ask this like your opinion would matter to me. It does not. Or perhaps it does. This is a recount full of contradictions and perhaps you will embrace them or reject them.

I had been wandering about in Roberta's flat, going through her things. I had slept in her bed next to her and she had been unaware of my presence. I had even stroked her body and whispered into her ear without her knowing. She was oblivious to my existence. I wanted her to notice me. I wanted us to begin a communication 'game' together. I could not resist her. I did not want to observe her, like I normally did, in the shadows. I had only exposed myself to a few Masters. I did not want to admire her from afar. I needed contact. I wanted her to be aware of me. I decided, against common sense, to approach her.

'Is there anybody sitting here?' I asked her. She did not look up. It was a line. She did not need to see me to know that. She just had no idea how significant the line was and who it was from.

'Obviously not,' she replied to the empty chair. I liked her a lot. She was broken. This was my favourite type of woman and I had broken her. My ability to destroy human hearts and minds pleased me greatly at times. You will probably feel anger when you read that line. I hope that you do or it will make you as terrible as me.

'Then I shall sit down,' I decided, finding the seat. She did not reply.

Roberta concentrated on the paper. This novel was not

even a sixth finished and she was all out of creativity already. She may have inherited her mother's nose but that was where the comparison ended. Her mother could write in such an effortless fashion for days on end. It used to exhaust me watching her. Roberta could not even 'feel' that she was creating a literature classic. I knew before her. I smiled to myself at this fact.

I was amazed by the likeness of mother and daughter Downs. Roberta had Willow's long flowing brunette locks and that determined expression that I had gazed at for so long from afar. Willow had fought me desperately when I took her pineal gland. She had ripped into my hair and skin. She had not wanted to die because of her child but die she did. I was undefeatable.

I smiled again as I watched how Roberta was determined not to make eye contact with me even though she wanted to. I knew her more than she knew herself.

'What are you writing?' I asked, knowing exactly what she was writing. I could see the words before she could form them in her mind. I have to humour myself though. I have to find a starting point for conversation. She did not reply.

'I have a feeling that this will be the work that makes you,' I said. I knew it would be the work that would make her, if she completes it of course. I had little faith in her finishing it with her current state of mind. She had the talent but she did not have the same work ethic as her mother.

Roberta was listening to me but she did not reply. She wished for me to go though she was not sure why. It was obvious and yet I stayed.

'Words are like thunderstorms. You fear them but when they come they are so refreshing and exhilarating, do you not think?' I said.

'I hate storms,' she replied quickly. This surprised me. She had been so composed until that moment and I was expecting nothing from her mouth.

'Then you hate life,' I decided.

'Please go away,' she said.

'As you wish,' I said.

I pushed the seat away from the table in a dramatic fashion. It was a deliberate act of displeasure though I did not care if I stayed or not. She was mine and always had been. Even before her birth I had claimed her. Despite her aloofness I knew that she wanted to engage with me. I could wait. I was the hands of time.

I left the cafe. Roberta looked up and immediately glanced towards the windows filled with offers and adverts. She was searching for me. I did not have to see her to know her actions. Still, I turned and saw her. Our eyes locked. I held her stare for as long as the windows would let me. Then I was gone.

For some time, Roberta kept staring at the windows,

waiting for me to return. I would not. She would have to wait for me. She looked back at her paper. She wrote on the empty page 'Words are like thunderstorms'. I had her. It was so easy.

3. Reflecting on my existence

Please do not ask me what I am about for I have no response to satisfy your curiosity. As I said before, I do not have a lot of answers.

My first memory is of sand in my eyes and a man in a white robe placing his hand to my head and smiling in a weary fashion. It is a smile that knows the truth. It is an expression that says 'Everything will be ok' but the eyes are screaming 'No, it will be far from ok.'

I was not born. I feel sure of this. I cannot relate to the experience of labour. I feel nothing when I see a child being born. Not fear, not disgust, not love. I have no opinion on the matter though I have walked maternity wards trying to understand the process and the effects that it has on humans.

I have no memory of a mother or father. I only remember the man in the white robe. Nobody has ever tried to 'claim' me. I have never tried to find somebody. Well that is not quite true. I must remember to try to be honest. I have been searching for something, just not someone in particular. I have observed the human race for centuries and the interactions that I have witnessed do not resemble the 'life' that I have at all. I am unique as far as I know.

The man in the white robe took me under his wing. He never spoke to me, not once in the whole time that I spent with him. How long this was for I do not know but it must have been over several years for I watched him age like you humans do. His dark hair turned grey, his eyes grew dimmer and his mouth more refined. His face started to crease and his teeth began to fall out. It was terrifying to watch for I could not understand what was happening to him and he could not tell me. It is only over time that I have learnt that he simply aged. It is a natural process for human beings and yet to me it was horrifying to behold. I cannot age. Again to this day I do not understand why but trust me when I tell you that I have tried to understand why.

And when time had ravaged him and had his fill of him, time simply let him go. He died in my arms. I was not sure how to feel when he stopped breathing. At first I thought that he had fallen asleep. It became obvious to me, eventually, that something had changed in him and that he was not going to wake up again.

There was no ceremony for him. I have since learnt that many humans like funerals to honour their dead. It had been only the two of us so I had nothing to compare us to. I was not sure what to do with him in death.

I held his lifeless frame for the longest time until he grew stiff and cold. Then his colouring changed and he started to smell of death (a smell that I have become familiar with) and I knew, instinctively, that I had to let him go.

I placed rocks in his clothing and let the river have him. I watched as, at first, his corpse seemed to fight the ripples that would bury him. Then he simply faded away from me, inch by inch, until the river had consumed him.

I never knew his name. He never had a grave. There are no remaining traces of his life. Nobody would remember him apart from me. Nobody would come across his tomb and read his name and life span. He had dissolved in the water and his bones lay on the bed now.

I wandered for a time after that. I knew that I could not stay where I was now that I had lost him. I walked for days, living off the hospitality of strangers, mainly women, for I was supposedly a 'handsome' man. Casual sexual encounters for money and a place to stay became my way of life. Women can be vulgar in the sexual sense. Not all of them are innocents, waiting to be deflowered. I was, for want of a better word, a male prostitute I guess. Women 'wanted' me but I was not sure if I wanted them or if I wanted men. I think, as I sit here reflecting, I wanted neither until her.

I knew not my age or purpose in life but I knew that I was not like other humans. I exhibited qualities that were non-human. For instance, I could not drown. I tried it once, in my desperate days, and found myself swimming underwater like a fish for hours. I danced with a manner of all sea life on the bed and only came up when I grew tired.

There were other times when I wanted to end my life. As the decades became more technologically advanced there were more opportunities to do this.

Once I threw myself in front of a train but the train went right through me like water through a hand. The driver's face was quite a sight to behold. The colour drained from him and he had let out a silent scream as impact came near. I cannot tell you what his expression was once he had 'passed' through me but I can only imagine that it was one of complete and utter confusion and terror.

4. Paris to Kent - 1865

It was on a train that I observed one of my Masters, a great writer. As fate would have it, we ended up in a train crash together that we both survived. (I survived because I could not die and he survived because he was lucky).

I was sitting in his carriage and I was staring at him and he was staring back at me like he knew what I had come for. He had the eyes of a man who was expecting something and believed that it had arrived. I had tipped my hat at him in acknowledgment and he had nodded back at me. Contact with a Master is delicious sometimes. The most insignificant interaction can elevate my soul for days, just knowing that a man responsible for such a body of work felt me worthy of a nod. Although I had made my presence known to him, I had not conversed with him. I had learnt from my favourite Master, that it was not wise to become too familiar with your kill. A polite tip of a hat was not breaking this rule.

We were travelling first class, of course, as by now I had amassed a fortune for myself of which how I will not go into now. I was sitting in my plush seat staring out of the window when all of the other carriages started to slope off the bridge that was being repaired, like lemmings to their death.

There was panic, screaming, emotion that could fill the pages of time if necessary. I will not try to describe the scene in intense detail as I cannot do it justice. Imagine the end of the world. Smoke billowing, terrifying noises and then silence followed by howling, burning and blood. I could see even in the more frightening, uncertain moments that this Master's brain was ticking and writing fiction from fact in his head, the genius that he was. Not even the threat of his own life being taken could stop his imagination from coming alive.

Many people died and several more were injured that day but not us. How cruel to let me live when I ached for death and yet the lives of the unsuspecting innocent were taken away that day. How weird your world is.

Let me tell you something about this Master. I knew that he would stay in the aftermath of the crash and tend to the injured. That was the reason why I had decided to let him live just then. It would have been callous to kill a man with such spirit and he was still working on an unfinished manuscript. In fact he had to go back to get it as he left it on the tracks.

Still, I killed him too soon. I needed his essence. I knew that he would taste and feel divine for he had known suffering and pleasure in equal measure.

He would never reveal his past though. It lurked in the

shadows like a terrible dark secret. He was living in a time when a tainted past could affect your future and so he buried it deep in the earth of modern day, praying that it would not rise.

I used to watch him sometimes. I would flit in and out of his life as his family grew in number. His poor wife. She could not match this man, the never ending author with boundless energy for the written word. She was but a mere mortal like the rest of humanity.

'Why did you marry me?' she would scream at him sometimes surrounded by copious amounts of mouths to feed.

'I have no idea,' he would reply and place his hat on his head and leave the noisy house for the promise of a good night on the streets.

He would leave her standing there, in the ruins of their love, trying to understand how she could still feel anything for him when he was so cruel at times. Women are like that though. You endure a lot for men when they really are not worth it.

I was at their wedding day and I knew it would not last. They were in love on that day, I think, and perhaps for a few years after the wedding cake had been eaten. It was obvious to me and to him though that his chosen wife was not his intellectual equal. He made the simple mistake of marrying the wrong woman. Many people do this. I could go further and say he made the simple mistake of getting married. Masters should never get married, I believe. They should remain on their own; dedicating their heart to their work like a priest dedicates his life to his God. Poor priests. You are wasting your time.

The love of his life was denied to my Master for her parents did not see him fit or worthy of her. Did he ever get over it? Who can tell? Sometimes I can read into the minds of Masters and sometimes they are impenetrable forces.

What I can tell you is that he met the love of his life again much later, when they were both married to somebody else, and in that moment he realised that she was not the love of his life after all. That, like his fiction, he had woven a wonderful image of perfection and placed her on a pedestal. Or, like with all things, time eventually erodes even the images of the loves of our lives.

When his marriage eventually broke down, as it was always going to, I was there. I was hovering in the background, listening in like the unforgiving spy that I am. I was there when a bracelet was delivered to their household by accident. It was intended for somebody else but it fell into his wife's hands.

It was the evidence that she needed to confirm her worst fears.

'I knew that you were unfaithful,' she had cried, throwing the jewellery at him. He did not respond. He did not even feel that he owed her an explanation or apology. He simply bent down, picked up the bracelet and left the room. I watched as his wife cried enough tears for all of the suffering women in England. She had given her husband her body for child bearing and her mind for manipulation and he had grown tired of her.

On the odd occasion I feel guilty invading the privacy of my chosen prey and sometimes I love it, thrive on it in fact. There was no steam or anger to the demise of their marriage. They were already in separate bedrooms and their union snuffed itself out like a candle that was already flickering and about to disappear.

Of course divorce was not really an option for this man in his time and he kept her financially safe. I like to think it was because of his kind heart and not to relieve his guilt at having to accept that matrimony was not for him after all. She was devastated by the demise of their marriage and never quite got over the role of wife and mother being taken from her. She lost hope and purpose.

I was not there when he first attached himself to his 'close' friend who developed into his mistress but I bore witness to their sins committed in stolen, hidden moments. How they gathered those moments and turned them into a sculpture of the forbidden for the world to never see. I could not say if the Master's heart was in it or not but what I can tell you is that when his secret child, that she bore for him, died in infancy he wept enough to put out all of the fires that London could ever have subjected itself to. How his heart broke even though he had so many living offspring but then is that not what makes you beings who you are? Wanting what is denied to you? Life is cruel. Or do you make it cruel?

She, the mistress, was with him on the train that day also. They had spent a romantic break in Paris, as I had done myself. In between observing them I had danced with a few Parisian ladies and men and broken the odd heart or two on a whim. I do not see myself as callous though. I see them as dreamers, attaching too much significance to insignificant things.

The hand of his mistress had hovered near his, never quite touching, all the more dramatic for the absence of contact. I watched that hand and I looked at her eyes. I concluded that her heart was more in the relationship than his. I believe that his true love was the written word and the opinions that he could express through them.

I have become distracted. Where does this take me with him? I tried to take him on the train that day but I knew what he had in his bag and I knew how much he would help his fellow passengers in their hour of need. Some died in his arms and he died with them in some ways. I guess courage abandoned me also. It is never easy to take a Master if you really admire them.

I do not know what I was thinking at the time anyway, pursuing him to France, lingering by him, getting as near to his essence as possible without actually taking it. The temptation near drove me mad with desire. Sometimes the longing is so great that it consumes rational thought.

After the crash he was never the same. He left himself on the tracks tending to the wounded that day. The man who went home with his mistress was not the Master who was. It was as if I had taken his essence that day and part of me wishes that I had rather than witness his natural decline.

He finished the manuscript and had started another which I did not let him complete. My favourite novel was the one that I wished him to go out on; his final unfinished one lacked something. I know the end to his last story for he had already written it in his head. I just denied him the pen. If people knew that they would pursue me for the answers. Let me tell you that the ending shall never be known. It is my property now and human minds will never know of it unless I want them to.

For the last five years of his life he dedicated a lot of

time to public readings including travelling to the new world. Then it was back across the waters to England and Scotland and anywhere else he could read. And then his body seemed to cease. Yes, you could call it a stroke but I call it my handy work. On the exact day of the train crash, several years later, I came for him.

He wept when he realised why I was there and what I had come for. It was with tears of joy.

'You were on the train that day,' he whispered, staring into my eyes with recognition. I nodded in response.
'I have never forgotten you.' These were his last words and they were for me.

He had 'died' so many years back that he greeted me like a long lost son. He did not begrudge me his essence. He almost willed me to take it from him. Had it been a burden after all? This is what I call the 'essence debate'.

In the one hand you have the mind of a genius and your brain is the envy of others and yet in the other hand you have this insufferable life caused by the very thing that people envy.

His last thoughts were with the secret child who died and I understood why. For so long he had hidden parts of his life in the name of respectability and the hardest part of that to deal with was allowing that infant to die with a whisper. No calling out of grief for its' small body. A name denied, a grave denied. Just like the man who had 'raised' me. I myself cannot tell you where the child's remains rest. I do not know everything.

Sometimes he would stare at the ground intensely and I knew what he was thinking.

Every last tear he cried, as I began my process, had the child's silent cries embedded in them. It was a strange rush to experience as his pineal gland slid down my throat. It was agony and ecstasy rolled into one.

To hate your self is a terrible thing but that is the most prominent emotion I hold for myself today. I did not particularly like who I was or who I was developing into. What was the purpose of my life apart from to kill? What purpose is there in that? Was this my fate? Why are there no others like me? There were murderers. Your world is swamped with them but they were not like me.

Century after century I have tried to run away from my self-loathing but it always comes back, clinging to my body like a desperate lover. It is almost as if I need to hate myself to exist. I am not even sure how I exist. I came from grains of sand and was raised by a mute stranger who died in my arms.

Imagine a life like that? I am surrounded by life and people but I have no idea why or how. Only the Masters see the real me when I come to take their essence, otherwise to the person going about their everyday business I am human, just like you.

I have read books on supernatural beings like vampires (I do not crave blood or die in the sunlight) and demons (I do not invade the human soul or wish evil on anybody). I have scoured libraries looking for written words which will explain who I am, or what, and there is nothing like me documented.

Sometimes I go to the top of a high building and I scream out into the night, begging to know who I am, hoping that the stars may gather the question up and find somebody to answer it. Nobody has answered it. In the dark silence I throw myself from the rooftops of these buildings, knowing that I will land softly on the ground, unharmed.

I have worked my way through so many bars and alleys looking for my kind. I would like to think that I will recognise my species when I come face to face with them. There is no recognition. There is only my reflection.

And God? The God that you talk of? He is nowhere and never has been. I come from everywhere and from all time and he is nowhere. He never comes in the dying moments of the Masters. Where is his all powerful presence then? There is no God and when I think of all the terrible tragedies that are born from the notion of that God, it should offer release. I want no God and there is no God. There is only life, love, hate and me.

5. London - Present Day

'May I sit here?' I ask Roberta.

She was back at the cafe and so I was too. I was attracted to her in ways that I cannot explain. I wanted to have some fun with her and I could only do this by introducing myself. It could not be love for I could not love as far as I was aware. Could it be lust? Or was it just common curiosity? I only knew that I wanted her.

'Whatever,' she said. She had recognised my voice immediately. I knew her thoughts. She found my voice soothing and had remembered me saying that words were like thunderstorms.

'Still writing I see?' I said, ignoring her obvious rebuff. I knew that even though she was acting like she did not care for my presence, she cared greatly. She wanted me to stay. She had complicated feelings for men but she did not want me to leave.

She did not reply. She sipped on her coffee instead. I liked the way her lips made contact with the cup. I envisaged my lips on hers. I already knew what she would taste like, what she would feel like.

'So do you think that words are like thunderstorms?' I asked.

'No but I think men are.' I liked this reply. She was challenging me. She wanted to engage in some kind of war of words with me. I was a willing opponent.

'Why did you write it down if you did not agree with me?' I asked.

'How do you know that I wrote it down?' she said. Her voice was rushed and she immediately regretted her defensive response. She now looked intently at the face belonging to the voice. She had an immediate feeling of familiarity with my face that she could not explain or rationalise.

'I did not know but I do now,' I lied. I knew everything there was to know. It was part of my gift or curse. Label it as you see fit.

She felt herself blushing and put her head back down.

'Why are men like thunderstorms then?' I asked. She did not reply though she wanted to. I encouraged her.

'Come on, humour me. As a man I think I have the right to know why I am like one.'

She got to her feet. I thought that this action meant that she would not respond but she did.

'Because they excite and terrify all at once and all they bring are tears,' she said in a half whisper. She grabbed her coat from the back of the chair and rushed from the cafe.

She had been hurt. She was vulnerable. She was mine.

6. France - 1890

One of my targets never knew love. How love hated him. And I knew why. You have to watch a man day in and day out to get under his skin and discover his true being. He was quite mad. He was frantic with energy and driven by a frenzy that I have witnessed before in other artists. This man did not even rest in his sleep. He was a constant steady stream of unrelenting anguish and he poured it out onto the canvas. It was traumatic to watch at times.

Sometimes I used to lie next to him in the dead of the night and stroke his weary brow. He could feel the sensation and often questioned it.

'Who is there?' he would ask the emptiness of the room. I never answered. I left him to draw his own conclusions. It was cruel of me in some ways. I could have reassured him that he was not insane and that my presence was real. That I would not hurt him until the time was right and in the meantime I would admire him. I remained silent.

His debate over whether or not I existed fuelled his need to create and I did not want to stop this need. He would see me at the end though when I came to get my prize, after years of watching his genius blossom into fields of imagination.

What magic this man could weave on the waiting canvas. Once, in Arles, I sat stunned all day as he assaulted canvass after canvass with any instrument to hand.

It was exhausting watching a man take the agonies of his life and project them on to material. He was bearing his soul in broad daylight and it was difficult to watch, even for me who had seen enough anguish to last forever. It attacked my conscience and begged me to look away from the agonising display of human frustration and yet I watched, rooted to the spot like the voyeur I was.

This was why love remained a stranger to him. He was too much of a match for love. How can one love a man with his drive for tragedy? The everyday could not occur in this man's life and it frightened people. It frightened him.

How many times did I walk next to him as he institutionalised himself? Every step he took lead to the destruction of his freedom and the birth of captivity. The darker moments were awful and yet I thrived on them also because I knew that the deeper he dug himself into dark thoughts, the more vibrant his work would be.

Sometimes I would look in the mirror and see resignation in my eyes. The same look of resignation in his eyes as he placed himself into a terrible atmosphere with degrading and painful treatment to try and make himself believe that he could fit into society one day. Why would he want to fit into a 'society' not worthy of his mind and heart?

No man like him can ever 'fit' anywhere. It would be like trying to put a square into a circle. From the moment that he was born he would forever walk on the edge of life, failing at everything, even his own suicide. Well, I had a hand in that. He just would not stay still as I pulled the essence from him. You would imagine that he would have welcomed me with open arms for he had been spurned so many times. I wanted him and yet he fought me off like a distant lover.

There I was, on a hot day in France, wrestling with this Master's essence and a gun. It was not how I had envisaged it in my head. But then he had always been this electric character who was so unpredictable. What a mess. It tainted the rush for me. Masters should never submit and make the kill easy but at the same time they should never behave in a way that jeopardises the ultimate aim of the act, my pleasure and survival.

He vexed me much with his fighting display. He managed to escape from me and I let him. I knew that the damage had been done and that the gun wound would cause an infection to ravish his body. I did not like killing my Masters so if the odd one escaped to die somewhere else that was fine by me as long as I had their essence.

I placed the gun in my coat pocket and watched as he stumbled out into civilisation.

He did not die immediately. He died several hours later. His life dragged itself to the end in a slow laborious fashion which would have driven this genius even madder had he been conscious of it. He was a shell now that I had consumed his essence. The last thought he had lay with the son of ‘God’.

As he lay dying he thought about how he had ignored god’s calling and had decided to paint pictures instead of helping lives. He felt that love had spurned him because his life should have been a celibate one. He felt that the punishment that was given to him was harsh but he understood fully, in death, why love could not be his.

He thought all of this in a matter of moments. God was not in the room with him when that happened because God is nowhere and never has been. I so wanted to tell him that priesthood would have been a wasted life but I left him with his thoughts instead. I had got what I came for and it was not my job to reassure a genius in their dying moments.

7. London - Present Day

'Can we start again?' I asked Roberta, finding a seat at her table. I did not ask to sit down for she never really answered the question.

'I was not aware we had started before,' she said. In truth she was enjoying the attention from me. It had been some time since she had exchanged anything with a man. This was obvious to me. They always let her down in the end and the only man who she seemed to truly love was her father though even that relationship was complicated.

'I think I kind of started it and you ended it,' I said.
'Look, what do you want? I'm kind of busy here.'
'And yet you choose to write in a public place when you could write at home and have no distractions?' I said.

This time I had bought a coffee and I gently stroked the cup as I stared at her, imagining that it was her skin. Her skin was flawless and pale, my favourite kind of skin. Her eyes captivated me. They were just like her mother's. I put the thought to one side. I did not like remembering her mother's dead eyes.

Roberta did not like my criticism of her chosen work environment. She liked to be surrounded by life as it inspired her but she did not see why she had to explain herself to me, a stranger, and so she did not.

'I am Robert,' I lied. I had no name but Robert would do for the purposes of this conversation for it was the male version of Roberta. It was a connection for her to latch on to should she wish to do so. She did.

'Why are you so desperate to talk to me?' she asked. This was my third attempt and Roberta had given me no sign that she wished to interact with me, apart from the lingering gaze through the window.

'Do I come across as desperate? There are so many others I could talk to instead.' It was not a threat but it sounded like one as the words escaped from my mouth.

'Well go and talk to them then. I need to write.'

'What about this evening?' I said. I knew that she would agree. I could almost feel her yearning for me radiating out from her clothes. I intrigued her. The handsome stranger who seemed to desire her company more than anything else. It was straight out of one of the romantic novels that she despised yet being in one of those novels was such a more pleasant experience than reading one.

'What about it?' she asked. She wanted to play with me. I did not mind. I was playing with her also after all.
'I shall take you out somewhere. What do you like to do?' I knew exactly what she liked to do. I knew her every desire. She was my favourite film.
'To be left alone,' she said. She stood up. I joined her.
'It is fine. I will leave. You were here first. It is only fair,'

I said, picking up my coffee. I knew that this act would impress her.

'It was nice not quite getting to know you. I shall leave you to your writing,' I said.

I stared into her eyes and I knew what she was feeling. She thought that we had met somewhere before, perhaps in a previous life. She recognised my features and it was driving her to distraction. How could she ever get to solve the mystery if she did not allow our communication to continue?

I turned and started to walk away.

'I like Italian food,' she said after me. It was all so effortless. I stopped in my tracks and smiled. I turned around to face her.

'Italian it is then. Shall I meet you here? Seven?'

She nodded.

'I will not wait for you if you're late though. I'm not the kind of woman who waits,' she said. I knew that already.

'I had better not keep you waiting then,' I decided and left her at her familiar table.

She watched me as I left the cafe and disappeared from her view. I would have her. I would make her want me and then I would destroy her all in the name of creativity.

8. London – 2010

Of course present day London is not the first time that I have visited this magnificent city and tasted all of the delights that it has to offer. Through the centuries I have been to London many times and killed many Masters here.

In 2010 I took a Master who was the toast of literature town. His fifth and what was being billed as 'the work of his life' had been nominated for every literature award going. His stories weaving webs of how women had always fought to abandon the margins of life were being devoured by woman across the globe. A strange devouring when you consider that the person that these women were seeking salvation in was from the same species that placed them in the margins in the first place.

I am of course talking about 'man'. Man, the creator of his own destiny, the back turner on Gods and demons alike. The species that can outdo all species, or at least thinks he can, until one day when his own creations will turn their backs on him.

This is not a history lesson though or a walk in gender war territory. This is about a Master and the night that I took his life force from him like it was nothing but a passing moment. I must tell you that to end the life of somebody is not an easy thing to achieve. It is, if you have no conscience, but when conscience is your best friend, taking a life will keep you in nightmares forever. I am somewhere between that conclusion I like to think. I do not always want to take lives.

I had been watching this Master since he was thirteen years old. That was the first time I got the 'calling' for him. You can sniff out the Masters quite early in life if they are phenomenal. I had to be at Mozart's birth for he was born a Master. When he took his first breath I knew that I would be the reason that he would take his last. I could not let him finish, 'Requiem'. It was too breathtaking to complete. I had to have him as he created it. I just had to.

I took Beethoven's life force also. When I listen to 'Moonlight Sonata' it often brings me close to tears. Such beauty and tragedy combined into every note.

When you look back on history and you see the ambiguity surrounding Mozart's death or Beethoven's death there is a reason for that. I did it. I took them both even though one was buried a commoner and the other a king. They both died at my hands.

I have taken many musical figures over time. Any musicians who have been found dead in bath tubs or choking on their own vomit have died at my hands. I am not proud of this fact, well perhaps just a little. It is always so difficult to kill a Master of music though. Take away my sight, take away my voice but do not take away my hearing.

This Master entered the teenage world like no other for while most of his friends were getting drunk for the first time and experiencing the delights that their peers had to offer, he was shunned. His face was deformed and his character with it. There is nothing like consistent verbal torture to chip away at your esteem. He sought solace in a fantasy world of books and slowly began to realise that by not being accepted as a man he was in the same domain as a woman, as a lesser, as an 'other'.

And now at his fifth and final book (he has notes for his sixth one but he is never going to write it) I come in. I come in like the air from the window on a cold day. The Master shudders for he thinks it is a cool breeze. He does not know that I am in the room with him. I always study the faces of my Masters before I take them. He has a contented face at present and shall I tell you why?

Imagine this. Imagine that you are the child at school who is the 'nobody'. People have tired of battering you day after day for your misshapen face and so you have become background music. You flit in and out of the crowds like a discarded whisper. Then many years later you are the music. You play life how you want to. Your face may be disfigured but your life is perfect and the people who made your life hell now have their own hell to deal with.

The Master had just come back from a book signing and the girl who had rejected him at school had stood in a queue for his signature for two hours and then asked him to go to dinner. He got to reject her just like her rejection had haunted him throughout his life.

I know what you are thinking. It was cruel to take the Master's life as he reaped the benefits of his artistic ways but I was hungry. Not just hungry, I was desperate. I needed his essence to regenerate. If I did not take him I was sure that I would die and I am never going there. He was the chosen Master for that year. I could not back out. There was, of course, a substitute Master. There always was though Masters were becoming harder to seek out. I did not want her though. I wanted him. His tragic life was intertwined with mine. We were both living on the edges of life, ghosts on the peripheral landscape. I knew that the rush would be all the more vibrant for that fact.

It was the longest I had gone without a Master's essence and I could feel the life draining from my body. My blood was slowing down, my bones were becoming heavier. Every move I made was coated in cement. Why should I potentially die when the man who I had watched so lovingly for all of this time could save me? I had watched this Master since he was thirteen and now

I too was going to reap the benefits.

His end had arrived. The pineal gland is about 8mm and that 8mm keeps me alive. If you did an autopsy on all of the Masterpiece creators in life you would find either the pineal gland missing (due to my work) or if it is there (because they died before I could have them), non-calcification of this gland.

You see when it calcifies it kills the third eye of the human in my opinion. It is the part of humans that takes you to an enlightened state. The part that allows you to see things as they truly are and not the contrived conditions you humans find yourselves in. It separates the sheep from the shepherd, to make it simple.

The philosopher, Descartes, called the gland the 'principal seat of the soul' and the place in which all our thoughts are formed. He was of course correct. Divine Descartes. I took him too. My coming for him confirmed his thoughts on the matter. I shall save the telling of that for another time.

If the calcification process could be stopped, adults would not need to seek illegal substances to enhance their thoughts. They would have a natural high all on tap at their disposal. What can I say though? I have no answers for why your bodies evolve the way that they do. I am sure that the likes of Darwin (delicious Darwin) could throw some answers up into the air that you could be willing to catch but ultimately the knowledge is pointless. It will not stop the calcification process.

I place my fingers at the Master's neck and reach in with my 'imagination' and just pull out the gland. I do not know how this is possible without puncturing the skin and yet it is. I have come across spiritual surgeons who can 'operate' on people without even making contact with them. They place their hands above the individual's affected area and allow their surrounding spirits to complete the surgery. Perhaps it is similar to this. I do not know.

In that 8mm gland is the essence. It is that essence that allows me to live on. I will then slit the Master's wrists (my favourite form of suicide, so dramatic and colourful but it should never be too messy) and leave a standard suicide note on the side. People will question his death. His loving parents will say that they never saw it coming. His agent will drown his sorrows for losing his 'money man' and his fans will wipe away wasted tears. The girl that he said 'no' to might blame herself. Her presence may have triggered his past and the demons came back to haunt him. Whatever the reasoning behind his death, my result will remain the same. I get to continue living and would you deny me that? Am I not entitled to live too? Should this Master's life be more precious than mine? I have graced the centuries and danced with an array of historical figures.

The Master lived in just over two decades and never went to the dance. I think my life is more valid than his and so he is taken without guilt or sorrow but with the uniformed regularity that death has come to pass with me. It is wrong to say that for perhaps in some deaths I have mourned and understood what loss means. In the majority of cases I do not allow sentimental feelings to invade my heart. I need the essence. The primary objective must always be maintained. I need the essence.

Let me tell you what it feels like to feed and live on the Masters of the earth. A drug addict could probably give you a brief idea but you would have to multiply his or her high by infinity. And multiply the comedown by that also with reluctant hidden guilt. Only the junkie dies for his habit but somebody has to die for mine and it is never going to be me.

When you have the pineal gland in your hand it is like the tablet of all of the desires and hopes in the world encapsulated in one form. There is a moment where it sits in your hand and you stare at it. It is like Eve's apple (if you believe in that Bible nonsense). It is the forbidden fruit. You know that the consequences will be dire but the consequences are worth it to have your eyes that little bit more opened. I thought my eyes could not open any more but they do every time. A day will come when surely there will be nothing left to see or feel? It has not come yet though. Perhaps when I achieve the ultimate experience, via an essence, I will pass on then. Pass on to where though I have no idea.

This Master was no different. I stared at his 'tablet' for one second more before placing it on my tongue and then swallowing. It is a weird sensation. It burns my throat at first but then a 'freeze' effect starts to occur and my mouth goes numb. I fall to the floor and start to spasm gently and then my body goes into a state not uncommon to rigor mortis. Then the true journey begins.

I see the Master in the womb, in the pram, taking his first steps. I see him growing up to hate himself and his face. He had no mirrors in his house. They were banned but I can see him staring in one every night that he kept under his bed. I see him kissing his reflection. These are the things that only I and the Master will ever see.

Like all Masters I can see a pink glow around him at all times. That is the colour of the Master's essence. All this I can see flashing before my eyes. My mind is in overdrive and my body is dead. Feelings that cannot be described invade my still body and as I see the last word being written on his Masterpiece my body shocks itself into action. Then what can only be described as a powerful orgasm assaults my senses and it is over.

I lie there breathless. Living the life of a man or woman in one moment is exhausting for the body and mind. I feel woozy and disorientated. My body betrays me as I try to stand. I cannot find my feet and so I just lie there thinking of nothing. Then I forget everything that I have just seen. Regeneration is about renewal and the burying of the old and my regenerations are no different.

After feasting on the Master I know that I have another year of relaxing again. I am forever on the lookout for the next Master but the urgency to consume an essence has gone for now. Such feelings have been described as love by the greatest poets of our time (yes, I have feasted on some of them also) but I believe that I am incapable of love. I am not sure what I am or how I came to be but I feel certain that love is not an emotion I am capable of.

I had loved a writer once but not in the sense that intimacy would enter the arena. That 'love' had been fleeting and a mutual respect for a meeting of minds. No other love was possible in my mind for I had walked the centuries, sat under the stars and nobody had ever made me feel what was considered love. The regeneration feelings were as close as I had ever come or would come I believed. Until thoughts of her come to my mind, thoughts of Roberta Downs.

9. London - Present day

I sit in an Italian restaurant with my potential next Master and realise that perhaps I am capable of love after saying all of that. Forgive my narrative. At times I will contradict myself. This will be hard for you but not as hard as it is for me relaying it. The more I say, the more I realise that I do not know myself at all.

I have feelings for this woman that I cannot properly describe. I constantly want to touch her. I want to run my hand along her skin. I already know what it will feel like. I want to place my face against her hair and feel the softness of it. I even want to confess to her what I am but know that I cannot. The consequences of revealing my true self to her would be insurmountable. Especially if she knew that I was the one who took the life of her own mother. Besides what is there to tell? I am not sure what I am.

I wish that I felt for her like I felt for most of the others, a feeling of nothingness really except for the desire of the essence and an admiration for their work. This 'something' could be the end of me. I did not really have a substitute Master in place if I could not carry out the essence enhancing act on her. This decade was a bit wanting of Masters. I wanted her so much. I ached for her essence. I ached for her. Could I not have both? Could I not have her essence and yet she still live?

'So what do you do for a living?' she asked me. She could not quite look into my eyes. She focussed on everything but my gaze. She stared at the candle wax burning away. She stared at all of the paraphernalia that suffocated the low lit room. She stared anywhere but directly at me.

'Come, Roberta. Our conversation skills exceed the likes of our occupations and hobbies. We are deeper than that.' I smiled as I said the words, trying to align my face with hers. It was difficult. She would not keep her head still. I unnerved her. This pleased me for she unnerved me also.

'What would you like to talk about then?' she asked. She was now looking at me and I could see that she was slightly annoyed with me for not playing the 'first date' game with her.

I think you know what I am talking about. On the first date the conversation always covers the formalities. It is the physical curriculum vitae of 'mating'. I did not want to discuss such trivial things with this woman. I wanted to rip open her soul and set up home in it. I did not want to discuss work. Besides what would I tell her? I kill masterpiece creators for their life force, including your mother?

'You. I would like to talk about you. What are you writing Roberta?'

'I don't like discussing my work. I think it jinxes it to

discuss it before it is finished.'

I could not contain the small laugh I had at this idea.
'Nonsense. A true masterpiece cannot be jinxed,' I said.
'Maybe not, but a mediocre novel is jinxed before a chapter is even complete.'
'Ah I see. So you think that your work is mediocre?' I asked.

Her gaze left me as the word 'mediocre' came out of my mouth. She stared out of the window into the night. She rubbed her arms with her hands, like she was cold.

'I didn't say that.' She did not look at me though. Her reply met her reflection in the window.

The waitress placed a bottle of wine in front of us with two glasses. I smiled at her as she poured a little wine in the glass for me to taste. I would play this game. I sipped and nodded my head.

'Wonderful,' I said. The waitress smiled at my response. She filled our glasses for us. She was too beautiful to be waiting on people. Perhaps I would have her.

'Anything else, Sir?' she asked. There were so many things that I could say in response but instead I remained silent and shook my head.

She left us. I picked my glass up and let the wine slide

down my throat. Red wine was my constant friend throughout the centuries.

'Can I ask you why you write?' I said.
'You can ask but I am not sure that I have an answer,' she replied.
'You do not know why you write?' I said.

She shrugged her shoulders.

'I haven't given the matter much thought.'

'You haven't given the matter much thought and yet every day you sit and write in that café? Something must drive you?' I said. I watched as she picked her glass up and drank some wine as if consuming it would give the answer to the question.

'I'm more of a passenger,' she concluded. I was not going to let that go. She was a Master, even if she could not see it.

'No, I would say that you are definitely a driver, a confident one at that. You know where you are going but you have decided to take a detour.'

She smiled at my conclusion.

'You do not agree?' I asked. I ran my finger along the rim of the glass. She was watching me. I liked her watching me.
'I'm not sure. How did we get on to cars anyway?'
'You would not answer a simple question about why

you write,' I reminded her.

'Why do people do anything in life, Robert? There does not have to be a trigger. Not everything has to have an explanation. I write because...I don't know what else to do,' she said.

It was an honest answer. I knew her mind. I knew that she was floating through life on her back. She was not kicking against the tide. I was not sure if her mother's death had caused this personality trait but she was not swimming in the pool of life.

10. East Sussex - 1941

The stones are not that heavy on their own but as I add more to her previously empty pockets they start to weigh her down. This is the easiest and most difficult thing she will ever have to experience in her short, complicated and yet colourful life.

I wrote her goodbye letter to her husband. I wiped the tears away from her anguished face and she could feel my actions. Sometimes one can be so overcome with grief, or so underwhelmed as their life is drawing to an end, that the simplest of gestures are devoid of recognition. She recognised me and my gestures.

I can tell you some of her last thoughts as her feet paced up and down and she wrung her hands like she was rinsing a dirty dishcloth. There were so many things to think about. How many times had her thinking led her to her own entrapment? Her mind was her best friend and worst enemy all at once and yet how I wanted her mind. I wanted to experience the pain that she had for I knew that the moments of glory would be worth the suffering.

I wanted that mind as I carried her to the beautiful river that would soon take her body away from the world. I wanted that mind as I placed stone after stone into those deep hidden pockets.

One stone for her parents, one stone for the siblings who she loved, one stone for the siblings who she despised, one stone for the people who she could not live without, one stone for the people who she wished had never entered her life, one stone for her writing, one stone for her older better self, one stone for her dreams, one stone for her nightmares, one stone for the person she could have been. The last stone, which seemed prettier than the others, I like to imagine was for me.

She could have gone on, had I let her. She could have swept in and out of institutions like a graceful butterfly hops from flower to flower but I needed her now. Once she had finished her last manuscript and the war had done all it could to drain her of any last bit of positivity she could hold on to, I stepped up to claim my prize.

And what a prize she was.

It had been a short walk to the river that spring morning. I had held her tightly against me as I took in nature beginning again. Flowers were blooming and birds were singing. It was a beautiful day to die. Your protests will fall on death ears if you dare to tell me that I had no right to take her. You had not witnessed what I had. You had not seen the terrible sufferings that this woman had endured. What would you know of the night times that stripped her off her innocence and dignity? Have you ever sat and watched her brush her hair over and again as it was the only way to stop her smashing her face through the mirror? Strands of hair touched by the brush repeatedly so that she could forget about all of the other touches that she had experienced. Keep your protests to yourself. I had watched this woman for years and now this was my time with her.

Some are aware that I am with them. Some smile, some grimace, most look indifferent because they do not see or hear me. I am invisible to them until the end and sometimes remain invisible even then should I choose to. When I had gently covered her mouth, in her bedroom, she knew that I was there then. She knew before I covered her mouth that I was there. A woman with her great mind and intuitive ways is aware of everything and everyone. It was her curse.

As I carried her into the river I stared at her serene expression. She was letting me take her life so effortlessly. She did not fight me like Willow Downs had. This Master was tired of life, so tired of trying to be a woman. I do not know why I decided to treat her in death, the way that I did but I was drawn to the river and I was drawn to the stones. She would have the burial that my protector who 'raised' me had experienced.

I reached for her neck and drew out her tablet of wisdom and creation that I so desired and it came to me like a weak lion of the sublime. I had rendered her unconscious and now that I had what I needed I gave her to the water. She started to disappear. I allowed the river to take her as she saw fit. I could feel the water getting heavier for embracing her body and I found myself floating on my back to relieve some of the weight beneath the surface.

I could not see her at all now but I could feel her. She was in me and all around me. What an honour it was to spend the last minutes of her life with her. The world knew her as a writer and controversial character on the London set but I knew her as a frightened confused child who, despite huge odds, went on to write some of the most amazing prose the literature world has ever seen.

I stared at the spring sun as it could not blind my eyes.

My eyes had seen all that the world could throw at them. I saw her whole life and parts that she had even been able to hide from me. The last thing I saw was a lighthouse and the light on it that kept blinking in a hypnotic fashion that made me forget everything for a moment. The light was there and then it was gone. The light was there and then it was gone. The light was there and then it was gone.

When it was over, I swam back and stood on the bank staring out at the river that now held the body of my creative Master. Where would the current take her? Would she hold my Master forever or would she one day allow my Master to rise to the surface again?

You do not need to wait for the answer for this happened so long ago and, unlike a lot of my story, I can tell you the answers now. The river took her and gave her back again the following month. What was left of her was brought home and buried in her garden. Little comfort for her husband at the time but do not feel too sorry for him for he moved on as life insists. He fell in and out of love again despite what remained of his wife who he had dedicated so much time to. Humans move on. The only true love that humans experience is the love that they have for themselves. Everybody else can be replaced or erased in my experience. Do not allow love to consume you. Do not die for love for it will not die for you.

11. London - Present Day

'Do you drink coffee?' she asked me as she led me into her kitchen. It was my third 'date' with Roberta and I was now in her domain, in the official sense. I was surprised by how quickly she had allowed me into her home. I was also disappointed, if I am honest. After the rejection of the early days of our conversation I was expecting her to be more of a challenge.

'Yes I drink coffee,' I said as I removed my coat.
'Just place it on the back of a chair,' she said to me, pointing at the coat. I did as asked and watched as she went to the kettle and filled it up.

'Make yourself at home,' she said to me as she got some cups from the cupboard. As beautiful as I found her, I did not want to watch her making us a drink and so I turned my attention to her living room. I had, of course, been in it several times before. I had been everywhere in her flat, including her bedroom. I had even slept next to her in bed. I wonder what she would think of me if she knew this. I knew exactly what she would think of me.

I picked up the photograph of her, smiling, sandwiched between her parents. I had stared at it so many times before. Her expression and her father's had never looked as happy as that since I had taken her mother.

I placed it back on the side table and walked over to her book shelf. 'Timelines for lines' was there. I told you, her mother's masterpiece was on every book shelf, including her daughter's.

'Coffee,' her voice said behind me.
'Thank you,' I said. 'So who is in the photograph on the table there?' I ask. I am terrible.

'Oh, that's me when I was a child. I'm with my parents.' When she said the word, 'parents' she seemed to flinch slightly. I was unforgivable at times.

'Where are they now?' I said. I took a sip of coffee. It was lovely and sweet, just the way that I liked it. She had obviously listened to how I had ordered it in the restaurant and had remembered. She wanted to impress me not realising that she already had.

'Sit down,' she said, ignoring my question. I allowed myself a seat and pretended to take in the surroundings. I knew this room like the back of my hand.
'You have many books,' I said.
'Yes, I guess I do,' she replied.
'I guess an author has to read as well as write.'
'I guess. I would not class myself as an author though. I have not even completed one book yet,' she said. Her voice was sad when she said this. I could see that her 'failings' as a writer were having a huge impact on her.

'Aspiring author then,' I said with a smile. She returned

it.

'So what do you do Robert? I still don't know and this is our third meeting, I believe.' She used 'meeting' instead of 'date' I noted. I also noticed that she was pretending that she was not counting the times that we had met. She knew the number just as I did.

'Does it matter?'

'Not really, just trying to make conversation.'

'Then ask me something more interesting like what my favourite sexual position is.' I smiled again but she did not return it this time. I could tell that she was not offended by my question. She was more embarrassed. I decided to answer her original question to clear the air.

'I do not do a lot to be honest. I was left a fortune by an Uncle and I am travelling the world with it. I guess, like you, I am looking for inspiration for something. I am not sure what though,' I decided.

'So you're rich. You don't have to work?'

'No. I must say it sounds terrible when you say it like that. What about you?' I already knew about her. She did not work either. She lived on the money that her mother's talent had left her. She was struggling to mimic her mother's talent but she had her modest wealth to compensate for this failing.

'Similar. When my mother died she left me her money and this flat.'

'A lot of money?' I asked.

'You could say that.'

'How did she acquire her money if you do not mind my asking? My uncle did it the boring way, via the stock markets you know? Was she a business woman?'

'No she wasn't a business woman. She was a...writer.' It almost pained her to say the word.

'Ah, I see,' I said while trying to contain a smile.

'You see what?' she asked. Her tone was slightly annoyed, as if my seeing was accusing her of something that she was not guilty of.

'I see why you like books,' I replied as innocently as possible. She went to speak and then hesitated. She drank some of her coffee instead.

'Did she write anything that I would have heard of?'

'Perhaps. Her most famous work was 'Timelines for lines'. You may have heard of that.'

'Heard of it? I devoured it. So your mother was Willow Downs? What a talent,' I said.

I could still smell the sweat of Willow Downs as I had taken her pineal gland from her. How her nails had torn into my skin and punctured it as she fought to keep me from her. She had torn at my cheek and ripped the flesh open. I ran a finger over the area now as I remembered. How I had stroked her lovely long, silky hair as I went into the rush of pleasure that I got from the act. I was turned on just thinking about it.

'Very talented,' Roberta said.

'I am sorry for your loss.'

'I'm over it. It was a long time ago. She died when I was a child. I hardly remember her,' she lied. She stood up. 'Would you mind going. I feel tired,' she added.

I placed my cup down immediately and walked over to her.

'I have upset you. I can see this. It was wrong of me to ask questions,' I said. She did not respond. Her silence meant that she agreed with my conclusion.

'It's not just that. I need to rest. I'm not feeling inspired of late. I think I'm just tired.'
'Then I shall leave you,' I said. I reached out and stroked her hair. It felt just like her mothers. I felt electricity flowing through my veins. I wanted to reach in and grab her pineal gland there and then but it would be a wasted act. The rush would be a second hand one. I had to wait for the pure stuff. I was a perfectionist junkie. Besides, I wanted to penetrate her more sexually than emotionally at this present moment in time. I could tell by the way that she responded to my touch that she wanted me also.

I leaned in and kissed her gently on the lips. She wanted more. I wanted more but I also wanted to keep her waiting. Suspended love was a wonderful way to inspire a writer. Once a writer fell in love, and that love was returned, they slept with mediocrity. She would have to suffer for her art and suffer I would make her.

12. Middlesex - 1727

Writer's block is a terrible thing for a writer to have to go through. It is the equivalent of unrequited love, of the stringed instrument breaking its strings, of the scientist not being able to find the answer that he or she so desperately craves.

I am not sure why I have mentioned science for that is a grey area to me and one that I avoid if possible. I understand science's place, I just choose not to visit there. A few Masters from the science arena have ended their days with me though. One man in particular had caught my eye and it was imperative that I had him.

I had watched him as a little boy born on a farm in Lincolnshire. He never knew his father so I could relate to him. His father had died before the Master could even enter the world. Still, that was more than what I had. He had lost his father while in the womb. I had nothing. Better to lose something than have nothing.

His pursuit for knowledge was a replacement for his father, I think. His nose was long and his temper short. His ideas though were incredible. I knew from the moment that he touched a blade of grass and said 'One day I shall tell the world that you are not green at all' that he would shape the world of science.

I plucked a blade of grass, next to him, and looked at it

and then looked back at him. He could not see me. He was humming to himself as he picked blade after blade and piled them up on top of each other. He was seven years old and already a genius flying under the radar, illuminated by original thought and being raised by the mother of unique ability.

I pursued him for the next seventy seven years. He was one of my longest 'stalking' projects. Every time I went to take him he did something else, thought another thought that elevated him to another level. I was dizzy just watching his brain tick. I watched as ideas poured from him like water from a waterfall, beautiful, natural and drowning the nation with every ripple of evocative thought. I knew the rush for me would be indescribable when the moment came.

He was not just about ideas though. He loved and lost like every human being. Even the Masters are prone to base needs such as lust and enduring needs such as love. I watched as his library grew from book to book, as his notoriety grew from insult to insult and how his fame spread its' wings like the most majestic bird and flew over your unsuspecting heads and out of your lives.

What a legacy he left for the universe. He had the burial of a 'God', for a 'God' he was, if I could not classify him as a regular mortal. If your feet find you walking through Westminster you may pass upon his resting place. You should stand and soak in his essence as I once did. Of course you will not have his pineal gland. You will only have his memory but bask in his wonder all the same.

His funeral would have occurred much later had I not taken him for myself. Death is inevitable but his came sooner than he expected though he lived into old age. It is never enough time though especially when you are in possession of a brain such as his. The need to think never wants to run out of time but the likes of me ensure that it does.

I had made attempts before to take him but they were thwarted. His will was strong and despite my assaulting him with sporadic bouts of depression, he held on to life like his formulas. I often watched him in his library. He would spend many an hour devouring the greats such as Descartes and his discourse on reason. Many of the creators of the pages that his hands ran over I had taken at some time or another.

This Master had other ways to pass his time when he was not reading. When they found him he was full of mercury. Some say that the mercury poisoning drove him mad, some say that the mercury was in his body because of his alchemy pursuits.

I know the truth. I had driven him mad with my persistent ways. I let him see me fleeting past him. Was

I the shadow on the wall before him? Was I the face on the rug when he looked down? Was I the pattern moving in the curtain? I was all of them and much, much more. I am not sure why I had felt the need to expose my presence to him so many times over so many years.

Perhaps because he was a scientist and focussed on what could be seen and felt. What could be heard and said. Perhaps I wanted to challenge the way that he looked at the world. It was science (him) versus me (art). Art won. I dragged him down to the floor of 'hell' for by the end he had lost his grip on reality, though he tried to remain dignified in company.

His essence nearly killed me for he was the thinker of his era. I overdosed on his thoughts and feelings. He was the man who made the impossible possible. He was the man who made science magic and for one night made me realise what it truly meant to stand on the shoulders of giants.

Having said all of this it should be remembered that I am a tart for the arts. Science has its place and art has my heart.

A masterpiece comes from the gut instinct that was wiped out many moons ago by civilisation. There was a time when we were in tune with our mind, unlike now where the body matters so much more. We are in an age of instant gratification and so there is no room for a thought process. We have to be showered with celebrity and the flesh. Today materialism and business are the 'Gods' that the masses pray to. Something is lost but something is also found for some masterpieces have been created under such material conditions.

13. London - Present Day

I had told Roberta to meet me at 7pm in a London Park. I shall not tell you what one for should you decide to come looking for me you will spoil the haven that it is. Though how you would find me is quite another matter for you do not know what I look like and there are so many parks in this fine city.

I frequent this one often for solace and I do not want that taken away from me. I love parks for they are unaffected by progress. London is awash with unspoiled beauty if you can be bothered to find it. London at night makes my heart swell. It is a melting pot of nationalities and needs. I would overdose if the masses were all Masters. Fortunately for me, Masters were like unspoiled beauty in sprawling urban areas. You had to seek them out.

I was sitting on the bench waiting for my Roberta, for she was mine. I could have her whenever I wanted her. I will wait until I can no longer stand the urge and then I will take her in a common and vulgar fashion. I will defile her. My actions will only enhance her masterpiece more. I shall ruin her in the bodily sense to elevate her in the philosophical sense. It is the kindest gift that I can bestow on her. Perfect love from a perfect man will render her useless in the creative world. Suffering must be her bed partner if she is to succeed in the literature world and I know how to make people suffer.

'Have you been waiting long?' her voice asked. I looked up to see she had made a vast effort for me. It was obvious.

'I would wait forever,' I replied. See how I address her? Like a romantic hero from a trashy love novel. You women cannot get enough of this kind of conversation. Yes, you say that you have made progress, that the margins that you find yourselves pushed to by the male species are becoming thinner. Yet a slushy train of words can halt centuries of liberties and send them back to where they came from.

I could tell by her eyes that my words had had the desired effect. I handed her the rose that I had brought her. Cheesy and predictable and yet never fails. One single red rose. The most romantic and interesting flower in the world and the best image of love to be found. Roses are beautiful, dramatic and yet painful, if handled in the wrong fashion.

'Thank you,' she said, accepting the rose.
'Where are you taking me?' she asked as I took her hand.
'I have set a picnic up for you in a secret garden that only I know exists,' I explained.

She let out a small laugh. I could tell that she thought that I was joking but I was not. London was my playground. I dominated vast parts of it. I had many very rich and powerful women as lovers and they all knew that I was cheating on all of them. They did not care though. If you were lucky enough to have one night with me, for me to penetrate you, you would understand why they are so blasé at my lack of respect for them. When I enter you, centuries enter you also. I am all-encompassing and all embracing. They would rather have part of me than none of me at all. My 'night endeavours' were rewarded greatly.
'Through here,' I said. I opened the black Iron Gate with a key and led her into the picturesque grounds. The 'lady' of the house (I use the term loosely for in the bedroom she was exactly that, loose) was away and had granted me use of her house as and when I liked.

I had placed fairy lights everywhere, weaving in and out of the greenery. Dotted all over the floor were candles encased in holders and in the middle of it all was a picnic for kings. There was champagne and caviar to name a few things. Imagine it all and you will find it in this feast.

'I don't know what to say, Robert,' she said to me and this was true. My actions had rendered her speechless. I was slowly chipping away at her cold exterior.
'There is nothing to say. It is time to eat, drink and be merry,' I said, leading her to the blanket.

She smiled as she sat down. I got the champagne bottle and opened it. She jumped as the cork escaped and flew through the air to an unknown destination.

'To us,' I said as I poured the sparkling liquid into the flutes. She liked the word 'us'. It pleased her. You women are so easy to please, almost as easy as men.
'To us,' she repeated, accepting the glass.
'And to your book for it will be completed and it will be a masterpiece,' I said before taking a sip of champagne.
'I'm not sure about that,' she replied. Her response did not matter for I was sure. That was all that truly mattered.
'To the stars then,' I said raising my glass. I was so unbelievably obvious. She pressed her glass against mine. Her face looked slightly surprised as if I had said something that she had always wanted to say and had never told anybody.

She wanted me tonight but I would not let her have me. After tonight's magic I would ignore her for a week. She would not understand why but she would be able to forgive me for I had feasted with her under the night sky and kissed her gently. I had respected her. I had stroked her hair and told her that she was the feminine form of the constellations and she had loved it. No man had ever treated her the way I was treating her now. I knew this because I had watched her all of her life. I had tapped into her dreams. I knew that roses, stars and picnics were the images that defined love for her. My gift is seduction and I keep giving, when I want to, but soon she would know pain. Pain forms words like happiness can never understand. Pain was coming for her.

14. Michigan - 1986

The media and his adoring fans called him a genius which is always a dangerous label to attach to a person as you never know who might be listening. This Master did not know that I was in ear shot, that a careless word or two would draw attention to him and his creative ways. I normally attached myself to my chosen Master long before the Master manifested within the person but this Master was different. He was the last resort of my options. I felt uncomfortable swooping in on him and taking him as he was about to embark on a magical journey of drugs, sex and undying adoration but there was no room for feeling uncomfortable when I had to strike.

It had been a year since I had consumed my last Master and I was weak. My chosen target had died of natural causes before I could sweep in and take their essence which is why a 'Plan B' Master was always necessary. Some years were lean though and wanting of emerging Masters.

I could feel the life draining from me. I had gone too long without feasting on a Master. I could feel my blood slowing down in my body. I could feel my frame crumbling like a statue exposed to too many seasons over too many years, left unattended to rot as nature saw fit.

The 1980s were like a ghost town for Masters. There was talent but there is a vast difference between flirtations with creation and being married to it like a true Master was. I was a few days away from certain death (as certain as I could be) and so this Master would have to forgive me for bringing his 'bevy of groupies' lifestyle to an abrupt end.

In some ways it was his fault. He should not have made his first album such a masterpiece in a bleak musical landscape. He should have released an average record of lukewarm hits that gently nestled in the loving arms of banality. But no, his album was being labelled the album of the decade and this was just too much of a rush for me to pass up on and, like I said, I was desperate.

I always hate taking the life of a musician as music lifts my spirits in a way that no other creative medium can. I have killed many musicians and 'cherished' the rush that their essences have given to me in the moment when I turn life's sound down for them. Sometimes a musician had to suffice though. I tried to avoid them for they were my favourite kind of people.

I followed the Master into the bathroom. Nobody really saw me as I moved in and out of the crowd leaving no residue, no reminder that my presence was ever there. Despite him being a musical genius he was very much the predictable 'victim' of fame. I had lost count of the number of times that I had witnessed a musician dancing with cocaine on marble floors and on toilet seats with effervescent lighting. I was disappointed that he was indulging in such predictable behaviour but even the genius kind among you lack originality when it comes to decadence.

I allowed him his high (for mine was to come and it was only fair) before reaching towards his neck to carry out my own familiar drug ritual. With his gland removed, I stabbed the side of his neck and allowed the blade to run across it. To this day I do not know why I chose that violent method of death for him. I think, in part, it was because I was so angry that I had to take him.

His essence was one of the strongest I have ever experienced, in modern day, for he was still very much in the zone of his masterpiece and was experiencing pleasure as his essence took over my body. It was a potent blend. The illegal chemicals within him probably added to my rush also.

It was strange for me to fall to my knees and then on to my side to allow my body to stiffen and to succumb to the effects that the pineal gland of this Master promised me. As I experienced my high I looked into his dead eyes. What did I see in those vacant pupils? Death? Nothingness? I hate when I meet their gaze for a moment and they return it with those weightless, lifeless eyes. I turn away from him and the bloody mess, and struggle to lie flat on my back, trying to stare up at the lights that are too bright for human eyes.

When they found him they concluded that he had cut his own throat while out of his mind on various drugs. Only I knew what really had happened. There was something in this Master's eyes that made me want to weep. It was too easy to snuff out the light of a man's genius. There was no struggle. There were no last dramatic words. There was only nothing. I am reminded of the time I took the life of another music Master and made it look like he had shot himself. He too had this Master's eyes. They glowed with wonder, surprise and above all finality but safe in the knowledge that their music would go on forever.

15. London - Present Day

I watched Roberta as she slept. I had ignored her for a week as I had promised myself. When she was not writing she was sleeping with exhaustion. My every day conversations with her to nothing but silence had had an immediate and strong effect on her. The words were falling from her fingers like rain falls in the monsoon season, effortlessly. Am I not kind? See the sacrifices I make to ensure that my Master feels inspired?

I lay on the bed next to her so that our noses are almost touching. Even when her eyes are closed and I cannot see their beauty she is still so enchanting. She is like a work of art. It almost pained me to look at her at times. I had missed speaking to her for seven days. I needed to rest by her for a moment. I was breaking my own rules again.

I could feel her breath on my face and I allowed it to assault my skin, to get under my skin. I imagined myself inside of her and how good it would feel. I had known this woman since she was an unborn growing inside of her tragic mother. I could not tell her this of course. She would not understand. How could I look so young and yet have known her mother? I did not just know her mother though, I had killed her. That is the kind of information that would never be welcomed with open arms.

I abandoned the bed and went over to her computer and switched it on. I loaded up her story and started to read it. The beginning was weak. I wanted to write notes of advice alongside it but this was not possible. I should not be reading it in the first place let alone correcting it. The beginning of a book is so important though. That hook had to be in place. It was what separated masterpieces from pieces. I should know. I had killed enough Masters to comment on it.

The body of the work was engaging. It had its 'moments' but in its current form it was no masterpiece. Did I have Roberta wrong? Was she not a Master after all? Was she only good for the promise of sex and not essence enhancing? Was I allowing my emotions to cloud my Master judgement? I had never called a person a 'Master' and had my decision questioned. Was this a first for me? I had nobody to consult regarding it. How I wished for somebody like me in situations like this. Sometimes I wanted somebody to confide in and to seek reassurance from. Loneliness is a terrible disease.

I heard a noise coming from the bedroom and made myself invisible to her. I forgot about the computer.

'What the hell?' she asked herself aloud as she walked towards the lit screen.

Her story was open for the empty room to read. She

looked confused. She was certain that she had turned the computer off. She went to turn it off but thought better of it. An idea had entered her mind.

'Mum?' she asked aloud. She looked at her picture and then towards the bookshelf. Did she actually think that her mother could come back from the grave and turn a computer on? But then anything was possible. My existence added weight to that theory. Perhaps I could take this moment? I could grasp one of her beliefs and capitalise on it.

I went to the book shelf and saw 'Timelines for lines'. I removed it and threw it to the floor. She almost jumped out of her skin. She stifled a scream. I held back a laugh. While she could not see me, I was not sure if she could hear me or not. I know what you are thinking. You think that I am an evil bastard and if I cared for her the way that I was suggesting, how could I do such a thing? I was helping her. Madness was a great way to get creative juices flowing.

She walked, in a gingerly fashion, towards the fallen book and reached down to pick it up. She stared at the front cover and then flipped it to the back. Her mother's face was smiling back at her with that natural charm that she oozed. Roberta stared at her mother's eyes for a moment and then she placed the book back on the shelf.

She walked over to the telephone. It was 9.30pm. It

was not too late to ring. She dialled the number and waited for the familiar voice on the other end to speak.

'Dad,' she said. She already felt better for saying the word. He was her confidante, if a complicated one. She was not alone in her suffering, like I was, and I envied her for it.

16. Italy - 1500s

He was in his eighties when I took him from the world. The world had not yet seen his masterpiece though they would argue that they had for he was responsible for so many 'masterpieces'. He had the drafts for the true genius to come but I got greedy. I could wait no more. I had waited eighty eight long years for him. I had watched him court madness and loneliness on levels that I had never known existed. I had watched him deny himself of the pleasures that he truly desired and turn them into works of art.

No, I had waited long enough for him and allowed my desire to beat my ideas of perfection for once. He would have lived another fifteen years had I allowed him to but I could not. I had never wanted a Master of the arts as much as I had wanted him and there was no god to punish me for my actions. No god that I had come across as of yet in that part of my life that I found myself living in.

How this Master made me feel. I shall never forget feasting on his pineal gland for it sent me into a feeling of euphoria but the come down was brutal with it.

Nothing really changes where human emotions are concerned. It was the 1500's but it could have been right now in the 21st century for base needs always had to be met. Centuries did not distinguish one lust from the next. Historians will give fancy names to movements but it is the same emotions that drive a thug to kick the head in of an innocent person that makes the artist pick up his paintbrush. It is that need for recognition. It is the desire to leave your mark. Some are more effective than others in the way that they shape history to suit their purposes. This Master would never be forgotten. If history got amnesia the memory of his work would find a way to break through.

I lay on the floor for a long time after taking him. I saw many wonders in his eyes as my body jolted and went into spasms. I felt like I could fly and I so wanted to in that moment. I know that it sounds selfish; to end a life to enhance your own but if you could only join me in these emotions. Lie on your back and turn the light off and then create a world that involves everything that you have ever loved or desired. Nothing negative can penetrate the atmosphere. All you can feel is a never ending orgasm. You have just experienced a tiny part of what my body and mind go through when I swallow a Master's pineal gland. I cannot give it up. I will not give it up. Even if my existence did not depend on it I cannot imagine a life without my essence hit.

My rush lasts for so long after taking him that I forget what I have done to acquire such pleasure. Then I am falling so hard back to the ground. I want to cry out in pain but I know that this will be a silly reaction as there is nothing to cry about is there?

With the taking of this Master a terrible darkness came over me. There was a black blanket, hell bent on covering every inch of my trembling body for how my body trembled. It shook like it was the coldest winter known to man as my bare feet walked upon the unforgiving, frozen floor. Then I found myself collapsing to the ground again. I felt fire, hands made of fire, grabbing at my flesh and pinching me in a motion too quick for me to stop it. Was this the nearest thing to hell that I experienced if such a place exists? Was it punishment for taking a man who had spent so many hours trying to depict god and his work and wonder?

My eyes wept and my hands shook as I fought to steady them. I struggled to my knees for I would not lie down and take this assault on my person. I stood triumphant like a piece of paper in a hurricane and if there had been an audience they would have stared in wonder and said 'How did he manage to do that?'

I was still on my knees though. It looked like I was praying and perhaps I was for I was locked in that position as if I had turned to stone. Everything told me that I should not have taken this Master. I did not know how this information filtered through to me but it did. Some Masters should be left alone as they are beyond reach and what I had felt was a reminder of this.

I cannot remember how long I stayed on my knees in that false form of prayer but I awoke on my bed lying flat on my back and with a feeling of fear still inside of me. How seeing his work can take me back to that state of pure fear where I thought that death was in the room with me but he was not for I live.

I do not think that there is even such a thing as death for I have never seen him in all the centuries that I have taken a life. No entity has come forward into the spotlight to share in mortality with me. All I ever really see are the eyes of the Masters that have an indescribable look to them. Is that heaven? Is heaven in the eyes of a human for they are the only things that stand out after my work is done?

17. London - Present Day

'Hello love,' Clarke said, embracing his daughter. She was so like her mother now it was hard for him to look at her some times. He hated himself for feeling this way. He should rejoice in the uncanny resemblance for it meant that Willow lived on through her offspring. He could not shake the feelings of unrest he had whenever he embraced Roberta though.

Roberta gave Clarke an extra squeeze. She was a daddy's girl before and after her mother had died though their relationship had soured over the years. The decline in their relationship stemmed from Roberta's need to be a writer more than anything else. If they did row over her chosen profession they made up as quickly as they could. They had learnt a long time ago that life can be taken away suddenly and they did not want to waste it with negative emotions. Still the negative emotions would find a way back in. It is so much easier in your mortal life to be discontented than it is to be happy.

Clarke closed the door behind them and led his daughter into the living room.

'Where is Susan?' Roberta asked as she sat down.

'She's at her sister's,' Clarke said. Susan was Clarke's second wife and though he had met and married her more than a decade after Willow had been found dead, Roberta still saw their union as an act of betrayal against her mother. She disguised her feelings as best as she could on this matter though her father knew her true feelings. Part of Roberta felt that, after her mother's death, the only female that her father should love is her. It was unreasonable of her to think this but she could not help it.

'Drink?' Clarke asked Roberta. She smiled.
'I'll have a whisky and coke if you have any, dad?'

She kicked her shoes off and put her feet on the sofa.

'That bad hey?'
'What?'
'Drinking alcohol before six?' Clarke said. He was not judging, he was just commenting on the fact. Clarke tried not to judge his daughter on most matters. Not since his wife had taken her life. He felt that his every day criticisms of his wife were somehow responsible for her ending it. He had no idea of the truth. Nothing that he could have said or done would have altered Willow's fate. Only I had the power to do that.

Roberta ignored the alcohol comment.

'How are things with you, dad?' she asked as she watched him pour a whisky for her and a soft drink for himself.

'Ok,' he replied, handing Roberta her drink.
'Do you think that...do you believe that there is an afterlife, dad?' Roberta asked. She knew her father's thoughts on such matters. He did not believe in anything like that.

'No,' was his obvious reply.
'I called you last night because something weird happened.'
'What?'

'My computer turned itself on and was open at my story,' Roberta said.

'You obviously left it on and forgot about it.'

'I don't think so, Dad. I can see myself turning it off.'

'Well sometimes we see ourselves doing things and our memories are wrong,' Clarke said.

'That's not the weird part anyway. Mum's book fell from the shelf, her last book.'

'Book falls from book shelf. Very mysterious,' Clarke said.

'I have over one hundred books on that shelf and mum's one fell from it. The windows were shut, there was no wind. It didn't just fall either. It was like it was pushed from the shelf. How could it just have fallen like that?'

'You probably knocked it earlier in the day and then when you walked across the floor to turn the computer off your body movement edged it off the shelf,' Clarke said. He looked worried. He drank some of his drink.

'I don't think so and now-'

'-stop, Bobbie. Just stop okay?' Clarke interrupted his daughter. He only called her Bobbie when he wanted to treat her like a child.

'Stop what?' she asked, slightly annoyed.

'You're doing it again ok. We're not going back to that place again ok?' he said.

'What place?' Roberta asked, knowing full well.

'The place where you look for the tiniest of things to

explain your mother and her actions,' Clarke said. He could not believe that he had found it in himself to mention it. It had been hard to watch his young daughter going through years of therapy to understand her mother's death had nothing to do with her.

'I'm not doing that. I'm just saying that it's weird that it happened. I was feeling down about my writing and I just feel that-'

'-I'm just looking out for you. I don't want you to torture yourself over your mum ok? None of that was your fault,' Clarke said.

'I know that Dad. I don't think it was your fault either...or hers.'

'Don't start all that again,' Clarke said. His voice was getting angrier. Roberta was confused.

'Start what again?'

'That it wasn't her fault,' Clarke said.

'It wasn't. She-'

'- there is no bloody shadow man. I'm not listening to this again, Roberta. It was bad enough when you were a child. I will not listen to it now that you're an adult.' Clarke got to his feet.

'Shadow man? Who is shadow man? I just meant that she was not thinking straight when she did what she did so it's not her fault either. Why can't you forgive her like I have? Who is shadow man?'

Clarke sat back down next to his daughter. He took her

hand and tried to remain composed.

'It's not a matter of forgiving. I want to understand. I can't understand.'

'Some things aren't meant to be understood, Dad. There are things I don't understand,' Roberta said.

'Like what?' Clarke asked.

Just then Susan's voice penetrated the atmosphere.

'I'm home,' she was saying from the hallway.

'Your wife's back. I'm going to go.' Roberta got to her feet.

'Stay for dinner,' Clarke said. He knew that she would not.

'No I'm busy. I'll call you soon,' she said. She put her shoes back on and left the living room.

Susan was not in the hallway when Roberta got there. Roberta was relieved. She did not like seeing Susan. It hurt though it was not Susan's fault.

She left the house and went to her car. I watched. I followed. I sat in the passenger seat next to her though she was not aware of my presence.

'Who the hell is shadow man?' she asked her mirror as she adjusted it. She was sitting next to him. It was me.

18. Yorkshire - 1848

One of my Masters was like a shadow, not quite fully formed in the opinion of many. She grew up with two sisters and a brother in Yorkshire in the 19th century. I knew that she only had one book in her, one that would challenge the idea of a reliable author and influence the likes of Wilkie Collins. Sometimes it was such an honour to be amongst the Masters even if they were oblivious to my presence. The world saw her as naive and unworldly but I knew the truth. Under that fragile frame lay a roaring tiger, crawling with a dignified pace against the rhythm of critics. Society and its' preconceptions hurt her soul at times but she always had the love of her family to seek solace in. To her, the human spirit could not be crushed if support, in the shape of siblings, stood by her side.

What a difficult age for women to live in. Ah but what age has it ever been easy for women to live in? I am not a human man. I am an outsider, a freak to your world. I live in the margins of life. I live in the darkness unnoticed. My circumstances make me understand the plight of women so much more than my 'normal' male counterparts. I have the male form but my flesh betrays the male psyche.

To society she had led a sheltered life and more often than not she had indulged in fantasy worlds with her fellow eagerly participating siblings. Her home was her school and her haven and she had her father's books to educate her to a standard that she saw fit.

The Bible and Milton fed her brain, among others, for these were the words that would shape her sentences when she began to put pen to paper. How many masterpieces have been born from the womb of religion? That provocative element inside of you all, that chips away at your conscience insisting that you accept its existence. The atheist may fight religion until the day they die and as they take their last breath he or she will let religion in. It is the stain of thought that can never be wiped away. There is nothing like religion in life. There is no physical proof of a god or gods and yet it has an impenetrable hold on the masses, a dangerous and violent hold on them. A man will kill for his god. A man will kill for somebody whose existence he cannot even verify. I will never understand it.

Her siblings were her only true friends for she found it hard to bond with people outside of the household. This shyness may have been brought on by the preconceptions that surrounded her.

I had watched her since the age of three, when her mother died. She was too young really to let it affect her but later on in life sometimes she lay on her bed pining for maternal comfort. Her father was a loving and understanding man but a mother he was not. She wanted to snuggle in the arms of her mother. She was not a weak person for wanting a mother's love. All human beings crave the love of the woman who carried them. Despite the lack of a maternal presence, that sometimes affected her esteem, she travelled the earth and learnt to speak in other languages to forward her ambitions.

There were so many questions surrounding the authenticity of her masterpiece. Many people suspected that she was not the creator of it for they argued that her lack of experiences in love could never have given birth to the emotional intensity in her book. They were wrong though. How society and its' critics are always wrong on that score.

She was not the first Master to have her authenticity questioned and she would not be the last. There is a literary snobbery that infects and continues to infect the arts world. There is this unproven idea that to be the Master of a work that changes the world; you must be able to afford the world and everything that it has to offer. The Masters who I fed on throughout the centuries included those who had come from wretched poverty. Hunger or struggling could create a masterpiece just as much as greed and privilege. In some cases it could create a masterpiece better. In my opinion, desperation is the key to eternal wonder.

I watched her weave each word and unpick unsuitable sentences like a fussy knitter would. The fact that she had not been tainted by real life intense emotions made her more qualified than most to depict it for life experiences cause subjectivity. How can we ever be sure that anything that we feel is genuine? What is the difference between a day dream and the everyday? Both assault our senses in the same way and are therefore as valid as each other. Such are the deceivers that make up my senses and yours, I would imagine.

The critics were wrong about her and even though her sisters did what they could to rectify wrongs it was my presence that truly brought her closure. I had come for the Master and had it not been her I would not have reached in and taken her pineal gland the way that I did.

What good is the pineal gland of a fake writer? What good is the essence of somebody who has never held the pen of genius? No, I took her pineal gland and I would not have experienced the high that I did had she been the creative imposter that so many people marked her as.

Yes, she knew I had come for her and by killing her I had made her feel alive for the first time. Her death gave her the authentication that she had always desired. She held her arms out to me like I was her longed for lover coming to claim her. She was cold, thin and frail as she sat in the arm chair desperately reaching out for me. The room was so cold for December was the month, if I remember correctly. Sometimes I am useless with dates. I feel sure it was the end of the year. Yes, it was winter.

What was I to do but to take her into my warm, strong arms and suck her creative life force from her? She had lived for three decades and had never felt as much love as what I had offered her in those final moments. The love of a good man was not her destiny it would appear though she had created a man that would live on through the centuries and be portrayed by so many. It was a beautiful and poignant moment but it was also a sham. The essence was what I held on to. Her body and heart meant nothing to me.

19. London - Present Day

'And where the hell have you been?' Roberta asked before slamming her house door in my face. I waited two weeks before contacting her again. She was so angry with her father and with my absence that the words for her masterpiece had been falling on to the pages in a rapid fashion. She was two thirds complete. I could almost taste her gland.

'Let me in and I'll explain,' I said to the wooden door. I did not need for her to let me in. I could get in whenever I chose to but I had to keep the act going that I was a mere mortal. If she knew what I was this delicious, flirtatious encounter would end immediately.

I could see her smiling face behind the 'barrier'.

'Explain what? That you're an arsehole?' she shouted back at me. How the insults had changed over time. The profanities had become more coarse and obvious. Sometimes I longed for an insult from a different century. One that did not use body parts or that was more than five letters long. I sighed.

I knew that she wanted to let me in. She had walked back to the door and had her head against it. She loved the sound of my voice. She could still hear me comparing her to the constellations. This comparison was my saving grace. She would break soon and all because I had compared her to the stars.

'I had a family emergency,' I lied. It was an obvious choice but I did not have to try too hard with Roberta. Her heart was already mine and she would need me even more now that she had had a slight disagreement with her father. She would need a male figure to guide and comfort her and who better than her mother's killer, persistent stalker and coveter of her pineal gland?

'What? Somebody else died and left you loads of money? I'm crying this side of the door for you,' she said. This is the Roberta who I loved to begin with. This was the challenging, feisty, sarcastic one. Why did men make sheep out of lions when they loved lions? Why did I feel I had to subdue her and clip her wings when it was her soaring personality that attracted me so much? And why were you women so eager to let men make sheep out of you? Shame on both genders.

'Not fair, Roberta,' I said, trying to sound pained by her attempt at an insult. It meant nothing, ultimately, to me.

'Fair? What would you know about fair? You can't go around treating people the way that you have treated me, Robert,' she said.

'But our last evening together was wonderful wasn't it? I can still see the stars and taste the champagne...let me in and I will explain all,' I said.

'Explain to that side of the door. You don't need to come in to explain. I'm not letting you in. I'm mad with you,' she continued. She was mad for me, not mad at me. I knew this.

'Ok, look if that is how you feel, I will leave you alone again. You are obviously too angry to see me anyway,' I said and pretended to walk away from the door. I could almost hear her rapid heartbeat on the other side, panicking that I was going to leave her.

'Wait,' she half whispered, half shouted, as she opened the door. It really was too easy. I had no explanation for why I had been away for two weeks, well not one that she would want to hear. I had been right by her side, tormenting her to help her with her writing.

She went to say something but I went to her and immediately started to kiss her passionately. I knew that this manoeuvre would make her forget the need for explanations for my absence. I booted the door shut behind me and started to grab at her breasts as I pushed her against the door.

'I am having you, right here, right now,' I told her.

She did not fight me. She let me take her and took her I did, twice and with no protection. She was reckless when it came to men and a car crash when it came to me. I almost felt sorry for her. It should never be this easy to seduce a woman. I had been missing for two weeks with no explanation and had fucked her twice for her trouble, once for each missing week. Instead of being angry with me she was making me dinner. She was beautiful but I found her behaviour unattractive. Where was her dignity? Where was the woman who would not even let me sit next to her in the cafe at the beginning?

This time I would go away for a month and would come back and have her four times as a way of an apology. I would sleep with a thousand women in between also and take all of my techniques from them and devour her body with what I had learned. She would hate me by the end. She would be sick from my erratic ways and this excited me. If ever there was an illness to fan the flames of creative thought it was love and all of the agonies and ecstasies that it could produce. I would make her hate love but she would not live long enough to really understand what that meant.

20. Denmark - 1875

I knew somebody who understood what it meant to have a heart not wanted. He was born in slums to a poor shoemaker and his wife, a washerwoman with a penchant for alcohol. She lived on the edge of her seat, bathed in superstition and it was her character that influenced so much of his work when he became older and could put pen to paper to describe how he felt. And what stories he wove.

His stories were the kind that would be embraced by generation after generation. Beautiful tales built on such ugly feelings that the poor author had regarding himself and the way that he looked. He was awkward in appearance. There was no mistaking this and his physical features caused him great anxiety. How people had laughed at him. Had they known what he could do with a pen in his hand perhaps they would have loved him more back in life's playground and perhaps not. Children are so cruel.

They were cruel to a man who could sing like a bird. They were cruel to a man who would be remembered forever for his mind. There are statues of him and his creations in his honour. When life treated him appallingly the good side of me wanted to step in and tell him that the future would love him and not to worry about present rejections. I needed his sorrow though. I needed him to be taken to the brink of heartbreak to create his illustrious sentences.

He caught my attention in 1828. I had been just drifting in the world really. My last kill had been in the winter before that and I was hungry for another essence. Yes, I found him in 1828 but I would not have him until much later for the man just kept creating masterpiece after masterpiece. His life had been so terrible, so cloaked in despair and anguish. Yet born from this onslaught of tragedy were his ever increasing works. I could only marvel at him in wonder as he went from strength to strength and I went from kill to kill. I welcomed his continuous masterpiece creation activities for I knew that his essence would be first class when I eventually took it.

But while his work and his reputation grew, his heart did not. He had such love to give but nobody wanted it. He was confused. In between creating his masterpieces he would question his own sexuality and the whole idea of love itself. I saw so much of myself in him.

Unlike some characters in his tales he never found peace in love or life. Many a night I sat with him and bore witness to his empty tears. Drop after drop abandoning his long, weary face for the floorboards. He would cry to himself, 'Am I not worthy of love?' Of course he was but most of you humans are awful creatures really. It is all about the exterior for you. You never look within, especially now in today's age where instant gratification fuels your existence. There is no time to get to know somebody's soul in your fast food, corporate world which is just as well as I imagine that a lot of you lack a soul anyway.

This Master embedded his voyages of self-discovery into all of his works, hoping to find peace in the fictional words that he could not find in his waking moments. I nearly took him in 1840 when unrequited love nearly killed him. It was awful to see a genius fall to his knees in despair and cry into the night, 'Let me die.' I could not take him though because he just kept creating a better masterpiece. I have told you before that there is no better remedy for writer's block than the love of your life spurning you. Roberta would learn this in time. I was kind, sharing what I had observed over time with future Masters. You may see it as cruelty but I see it quite differently.

I followed this Master as he travelled through Europa, Asia Minor and Africa, creating travel books along the way. As he wrote and rewrote his memoirs, I killed and killed again. What a miserable pair we made. I think the lowest part of his life came when he started visiting brothels. For the lonely man that truly is the end of the line. Knowing that you will never have free love again and that you will always have to pay for the company of a woman must be a terrible thing to endure. I never followed him into the brothels. I could not bear it. There is nothing worse than seeing a Master sacrifice his honour for the simple sins of the flesh. I could not tell you if he fornicated with these desperate whores or if he discussed the colour of the curtains with them. Knowing his hang ups in relationships it was probably the latter.

And when there were no more whores and more importantly no more words, I swept in to his room to take him like a beautiful swan.

He wanted to die. The chain that he carried around his neck with the words of unrequited love was becoming like a millstone for him. The stories that surrounded him were becoming painful reminders of the terrible feelings that he had to purge to get through the day. 'You have come for me at last,' he said as he lay there staring at the ceiling.

I did not say anything as I hovered over him for I felt my heart starting to crack. He even had the power to get to a thing like me. He actually wanted me to take him because for the first time ever in his life it would mean that somebody truly wanted him. I am not made of stone. I am not a good person. In fact at times I am terrible but certain voices and certain sentences can reach into my heart and squeeze it until I feel that I cannot breathe. This was one of those times.

Now and again I still hear his words and I still see his eyes so full of acceptance and excitement at my presence. How life must have hated him for he welcomed death with open arms. For that was what I was. I was death. Sometimes I hated myself for what I was and sometimes I remembered him and he made me hate myself a little less for I gave him what he had always wanted, acceptance.

He could not even rest in peace. Even his own grave rejected him when it was dug up years later to have bodies removed from it that had been placed with him to rest. I stared down at that grave through the worm eaten wood and to his bones to see the only reminder of the genius that was. I felt a tear actually creep down my eye as I hoped that he could not bear witness to this.

I do not believe that there is an afterlife and I hope that there is not. To think of him standing next to me and seeing the desecration of his final resting place weighed heavily on my thoughts. He was being rejected by the living again and by the dead and even his own grave. How could a man who created such beauty and hope live, die and 'rest' in such ugly, pitiful circumstances?

I threw an imaginary flower onto his open grave and closed my eyes and mind to it all. I may be a monster but I like to think that I am not a hypocrite. Your world is one long dance with hypocrisy. I despise you all for it. I am full of hate. I must stop writing for now.

21. London - Present day and a memory

I have five months to go before I need my next essence. To count the years not by a calendar but by your kills is a miserable life. This was not me. Yes, some Masters had made me question myself. Some had made me feel shame, made me weep even. This was different. I was questioning moments then. Now I was forever questioning myself and my actions. This self-consciousness would be the undoing of me. It was my own fault. I was letting Roberta Downs get to me. I hated her and loved her all at once. Yes, I think I may love her. Is this the love that the poets speak of and that I remain a stranger to? Or am I just in love with her essence?

The problem with the 21st century is that Masters are harder to come by. There is a lot of imagination out there and the essence of genius still walks modern day pavements but something is lost. I do not know what the loss is but it is there all the same. Is the world running out of Masters? Or is it me changing? Am I finding it harder to determine who the Masters are? Am I slowly dying? Dying in this 21st century where I am experiencing what I think is love for the first time? Am I allowed to experience love because I am evolving? Dying? There was nobody to ask. There was nobody to confide in.

Perhaps I should let the weak feelings set in and see where they take me. Let the year fade away without consuming a pineal gland, without consuming Roberta. I would expire. Or maybe I would change from an ugly duckling into a swan? Whatever I was I could become something else. Perhaps I would become human like you? If only I knew how it would end. I was not sure of anything though. I had never let the weakness take me that far. I always consumed before any real danger set in. There was always a gland to swallow. There was always creativity to consume.

I was thinking this as I remembered a writer in the last decade or so lying on her bed and smiling. She was the toast of the theatre world then. Three plays under her belt but her latest one had really put her on the playwriting map. This of course meant that I could explore her like a newly discovered country.

I was not sure of her at first. Her first two plays had not impressed me but her third one was the one that made me mark her as a precautionary target. You see I need many options when it comes to feasting on genius. Some Masters die at somebody else's hands before I get to them. Life is also the enemy of the Master, not just me. I had to keep my eyes and options open for unexpected problems.

Her mouth was beautiful. She was humming to herself as she looked at the ceiling with a picture by a famous painter gracing it. The painting inspired her. It inspired me. I had consumed the creator of it. If only she knew that I was here to consume her, perhaps she would not be smiling. Or would she? My actions guaranteed her immortality in the public eye. If I let her grow into an old woman, let her masterpieces crumble and decay with her, she would be buried a mortal. To take the Master when they are at their most shining ensured the memory of them would be preserved. This was the key to immortality. Yes, some Masters I had let live on and their work had not decayed with them but I always found that the world grieved a little bit more for the Masters taken in their prime.

She was in her prime. I studied her body and her perfect skin. She would know no wrinkles or other tainted flesh because of my actions. She would die smiling. She would be celebrated as a beautiful young playwright even though inside she hid such ugly secrets like all Masters. I can never be certain of anything anymore but I can always be certain that behind every Master is a grain of tragedy that grows inside them, silently eating away at them.

I do not want to mark this woman for it would be like defacing a vivid painting. How stunningly serene her expression is. I touch her neck ever so gently and start to force the gland from its position. She feels discomfort. I see this. Her eyes are widening ever so slightly as the gland leaves its throne and make its way to my hands. Her face is freezing, her mouth no longer smiling. I want to kiss her gently and tell her all will be ok. I will not let her live long enough to realise that I have stolen from her what makes her who she is.

A gentle hand covers her mouth and she cannot even fight it. I think she knows what I am doing. Some are aware and some are ignorant. I whisper words of reassurance in her ear, which I will not share with you, and I place her essence on my tongue as I feel her last helpless attempts at breathing being played out.

I lie on the bed next to her and allow her essence to do what it can. I can feel her youthful, perfect body engulfing me. I see many things. I see her being born, I see her blossoming into a beautiful woman but I see so much pain also. The sins that she endured for being beautiful play out for me. What a curse to be desired by people who should never want you. I can hear the blame being laid upon her for being too perfect to look at. I see her cutting her hair off, cutting at hidden parts of her flesh. I see many things and for once what I see takes over what I feel. There is no rush coming for me. I turn to stare at her lifeless eyes and the guilt consumes me. I have taken her like so many before. I could have left her smiling on the bed, safe for once, happy for once with fear staying outside the door but I did not.

'I am sorry,' I remember saying as I closed her beautiful eyelids. What was happening to me? Can I endure these kills if they must be like this? Before I felt that there was a purpose to this. I shared in their anguish but it was coated in their triumphs. I had the rush that dulled the guilt. It made me forget that I snuffed out lives to preserve and improve my pointless one. Perhaps it was good that the present day did not have surplus Masters for me to feast on for as I got off that bed, and had stared at that latest kill, I swore to myself that I could never eat again. But of course after that I did eat again and I would eat again.

22. London - Present day

I had left Roberta for a month as I had promised myself. I now had less than four months until I needed to consume her pineal gland. My disappearing had affected her badly this time. Much worse than last time. I had not been intimate with her last time. This time I had taken her twice and then left her.

In actual fact I had not left her side. I had watched her since leaving her in her flat that day. After I left she had showered, to wash me away from her, and then she had sat with a coffee reliving the pleasure that I had given her again and again.

She had not slept easy that night. She ached for me. She had imagined me in bed next to her, hugging her pillow like it was my body. By the time she had fallen asleep she had married me and we were now parents living in some idyllic home in the middle of nowhere. She was a famous writer and I was the devoted husband and father.

After two days of not hearing from me she was not too concerned. She had reconciled with her father, not completely, but the building blocks were in place. She had asked him about shadow man in a `rational' fashion and so he had told her about him.

'When your mother died, you thought that you saw a man in black, stroking her neck. You got it into your head that he had murdered your mother and that she had not taken her own life. The psychologist said it was your fantasy to cope with abandonment issues.' Clarke had explained it in such a 'matter of fact' voice to her. I felt this revelation required more emotion but he delivered the sentences like you would a shopping list. I was most disappointed to witness it, especially as it was about me, but then his wife, Willow, had always been the creative one of the two of them.

When it got to five days without hearing from me, she was angry. Everything that she did she did with aggression. Small things like closing cupboards and turning electrical things on were done with furious hands. Even plumping her pillow was a dramatic gesture in my name. She kept checking her phone (even though I did not have her number and had obviously never called before). She checked her email and physical mail. I gave her nothing.

I sat and watched with a smile on my face. It pleased me to know that my company was so desired and that I could end all of her suffering with a knock at the door and unclasp of her bra. For a Master she was an idiot. My vast experiences with the opposite sex told me that the cleverer the woman, the more the fool in love.

Two weeks into my being 'invisible' to her she had shed biblical proportions of tears. She was even two days late for her period and she was secretly hoping that she might be pregnant because that would mean that part of me still remained within her. In reality, stress had halted her menstruation flow. The mind is the King of the body.

I was so powerful my actions could even influence when she could bleed. She cried when she got her period. Having her period made her hormones and emotions even more unstable. A few times she even stared at the razor blade a bit too long for my liking while shaving her legs. She was shaving them in case I reappeared and wanted her. She held the blade near a wrist. I was ready to make my presence known if necessary because I did not want her to die when she was so close to completing her masterpiece. Was it just for that reason though or was my concern for her on a more personal level? She would only hold the razor there though and then she would continue shaving her legs.

Three weeks into my leaving her and she was writing like it was going out of fashion. The passion that she had for me, she transferred to words on paper. Her need for me, her ache for my presence, was creating beautiful sentences that became paragraphs and then chapters. See how I help in life? Coffee after coffee, curse after curse, the word count was getting closer to completion and then she would read and edit the whole thing again.

When she did not write she would read her mother's works for inspiration. She would stroke her picture and kiss the photograph lips of her mother, lips that I had denied her in real life.

One month into my absence and she was in the penultimate chapter in her head. She lit a cigarette in celebration of this. Then she put her coat on and decided to go to her cafe, our cafe, where we first met. So I, of course, followed and joined her. Now was the moment to make myself known to her again.

'Is anybody sitting here?' I asked. She recognised my voice immediately for she winced at the sound of it. She was not going to play games with me this time.

'Fuck you,' she replied not looking up from her paper. There were so many witty things that I could have said in reply but I did not say any of them. I just stood, staring at her.

'Or did somebody die again perhaps?' she ventured, still not looking up from her paper. She wanted to engage in conversation with me in spite of herself.

'I was sick,' I said.

Once again, an obvious choice but I felt that I did not

have to invent elaborate excuses with Roberta. I knew that even after my behaviour for the past month she would still want me. She was shaving her legs so that she could run them along mine again in bed. She was still very much mine. She did not reply to my false excuse. It did not deserve a reply when assessed.

I hesitated and then placed the rose down on the table. For dramatic effect I said nothing to accompany the gesture. Silence really can speak volumes if the timing is right. I just left her with the rose.

I walked out into the rain and I could hear footsteps behind me. They were hers. She was not finished with me. I turned to face her. She slapped my face hard. I loved it. This action meant that she was crazy for me. If she did not want me she would not waste her energy on me. She would have stayed sitting at the table and ignored the flower gesture.

'You bastard. You absolute bastard. Missing once, fine but twice and after fucking me? Who do you think you are?' she asked through teary eyes. Her fist hit my chest with as much emotion as she could muster. The Roberta who I admired was very much back.

'I thought you had died,' she managed to say before falling against my assaulted body. I wanted to say 'I cannot die' but instead I held her, pulled her to me. A thorn from the rose that she was holding cut my wrist. I lifted my wrist to my mouth and licked the small droplet of blood. It made me smile though I could not say why.

'Never do that again,' she said through sobs. As if she could command me.

I pulled her head away from my chest. I stared into her eyes as intently as I could and then kissed her with renewed passion Then I took her back to her flat and had her in any way I wished to for as many times as I wanted. I was torn between love for her fragile yet fiery nature and the essence that was rightly mine and that would be perfect once it had slid down my throat and I had truly consumed her.

23. England - 1980

I am reminded of one of the Masters now as I sit in despair with choices to hand. I am waiting for a solution to save me though one will not come. It is not a sign of weakness, to be indecisive. It takes great courage not to convict to one thing. Take religion. Religion is the coward's way out. Religion is the sole purpose that the meek amongst us cling to. When all goes wrong, turn to God. When all goes right, thank God. When you need hope pray to God. I do not wish to upset you but there cannot be a God. Or if there is, he remains elusive to me. For all the souls that I have taken there has been no presence but mine.

It is the brave man who has too many choices and cannot decide. The coward picks one and stands by it, even if it is the wrong one. One of my creative Masters made a bad choice early in life. He married too young, a cliché really. He did not marry the wrong girl. He should have married her when life had assaulted him enough. To dedicate yourself to one soul before you have even grown as an individual is always the wrong decision. Lust and want will grind down honest and truthful ways. This does not make you a bad person. It makes you human.

He did not stay with his one choice. He allowed his lips to kiss another again and again and what ecstasy and anguish it caused him. It fuelled the poet in him and killed the man. To have a conscience when there are too many choices will destroy you. His conscience was too strong to be ignored.

I used to watch him as a teenager getting lost in his idols' sense of fashion and sound. I would laugh at him as he posed in the mirror with his naked, somewhat scrawny torso jutting out with pride. He would sing to his reflection with a smug smile on his face. He knew what he would become and it was a joy to watch him in those early days, when it was only innocence and the smell of expectation in the air.

But how all that comes crashing down when success embraces you. There is no room for innocence then.

With success must come a confidence that can be mistaken for arrogance. He was still the naive boy in the mirror but another persona had to be developed for him to survive in the harsh world that he had always wanted to enter.

I was with him when his wife gave birth to their child. It was not the experience that he had wanted it to be. It only added weight to his fears for when he looked at the life of his child he realised how important it was that he stay alive. His health was not good and his mental state was poor. These were deadly conditions for an artist and slashed a survival rate in half but now he had domesticity at his door also. There was no room for the luxury of self-indulgence that depression insists that you entertain. His child was relying on him now. He hated her cries for they were the verbal warning that he had to listen to what he wanted to remain deaf to.

How he loved two women for two different reasons and what could he do about that? I used to watch him stare into his pint for the answer and when it would not come he would light another cigarette in vain. At times I wanted to make myself known and be able to say to him that he did not have to make any choices. He could carry on as he was. Why could they not make choices instead? His wife? His mistress? His record company? His band members? Why did he have to carry the burden? What is wrong with having a wife and mistress? Loving one woman was impossible and there was no shame in admitting that.

Even seeking the solace in the artists who he admired gave him no peace near the end. Sometimes you can go so low that nothing can save you, not even yourself. Where words once danced from pages to inspire him they were now just empty combined letters that mocked him in his darker moments. The poet in him still lived though. It was the only constant thing left in his life. He thought that illness and depression had gotten the better of him but they had not because the poet sat with a cigarette in his hand and it was the poet who remained when I took his life. I could have spared him the suicide, I could have taken him in a moment of sickness but men like him should not die 'naturally'. Their deaths should be as dramatic as their thoughts.

I have no idea why my thoughts have returned to him as I sit here alone. It was so long ago, some decades ago when my hair was longer and I smoked too much also. Perhaps it was because of the choice element. I have choices to make and so did he. Perhaps it is because I heard one of his songs playing earlier because, unlike him, his music is still very much alive today. Or perhaps it was because I was contemplating 'ending' my own life.

What am I to do? How can I carry on as I am? I am getting so tired of the kills that even though the majority of the time the rush is still amazing the guilt outweighs it so much now that all is nearly lost. I do not think that I can bear another kill with guilt but I know that I probably will not survive without one.

Perhaps I should take my body to the edge and see if I can survive without an essence? Could I keep hurting Roberta like this? I had left her again. It had only been a week this time so far but I had taken her so many times for so many days that my absence was unforgivable this time. She was editing her work now in between tears that I had caused.

The grief that I had given her would ensure a masterpiece but I was having difficulty accepting that I could take it. I had taken her mother. I had taken her innocence. Could I take her life also? I had broken so many rules with regards to her. I had never had a relationship like this with one of my potential kills. I was doing it to ensure that the essence would be amazing but it was having an undesired effect on me. My once absent conscience was winning. Was I in love with her? I pushed the thought to one side. This could not happen. I would not let it happen. Things like me cannot love.

Why was there no other like me to consult? I had always felt alone but never so much as right now. Where were my guardians to show me the way? There was nobody to confess to, nobody to share my burden with. There were priests in their little confession boxes waiting for the gullible to share their sins so that they could get off on them but I did not want to enter a church. I had to work this out for myself. I had to choose whether I should live or allow death in.

24. London - Present Day

I had started to see Roberta again despite wanting to do the contrary. I liked spending time in her company. I liked sharing my body with her. I enjoyed knowing that I could end it all by clicking my fingers. I had the power. She was my toy. She had simply allowed me back into her life. Could she not see how her behaviour affected mine? She was giving me the impression that I could come and go as I pleased and that she would always forgive me no matter what. She should have been harder on me, punishing my actions more. It was more her fault than mine that I treated her so terribly for she allowed it.

'So how did you feel when your mother killed herself?' I asked as I lay next to her after a marathon sex session. I could satisfy her all day if I chose to. Just when I had her comfortable, and she was lying in a daydream listening to my breathing, I felt it was time to hurt her again. She had written nothing for a week because I was here. This would have to change. Time was running out for me. It was autumn and I had a few months left. While the sex and intimacy were lovely, they were not a pineal gland. The present state of affairs would not keep me alive. Yet I also wanted these moments that delayed her creativity. I was confused.

Roberta had her arm around me and she removed it and lay flat on her back. My question had upset her and, rather than respond verbally, she had chosen to show me physically what my words had done to her.

'You do not have to answer. I am just curious,' I said, trying not to smile. If she could see my expression my delight in her agony would confuse her.

'Well you know what they say about curiosity,' she said and threw the sheet back, too quickly for my liking. She pulled a t-shirt over her head and left the bedroom. I spread my arms and legs out to make full use of the free bed. Let the creativity begin again.

'I am not a cat,' I called after her. There was no response. Silence was good. It meant I had hit a nerve and that no words could challenge this. I lay there for some time listening to the sounds that she was making. She was running water, perhaps washing last night's dishes or filling the kettle up. I did not want to leave the bed but I knew that she would not be coming back to it and I wanted our war of words to continue.

I got dressed and joined her in the living room. She was sitting in a chair now with her legs up on it and smoking. She was sulking.

'What did I say?' I asked. I knew exactly why I had upset her.

'It's just not romantic ok, Robert? Do you get it? You

shouldn't ask me things like that in bed.' Her voice was trembling slightly.
'I will ask them out here in future then,' I said as coldly as I could. I grabbed my coat of the back of the chair.
'Where are you going?' she asked. Her eyes were slightly desperate. I despised this version of her.
'I have got things to do. I am sure that you have to,' I said as casually as I could. I started to walk towards the door. I could almost smell her tears before they started to fall. She was not her mother's daughter. Willow Downs would have been attacking me now, ripping the hair from my head, screaming abuse at me.
'Wait...we can talk,' she said in a pathetic tone. She was walking behind me now, like a servant awaiting my command.

'The time to talk is over for now. It passed,' I said, smirking, as I unlocked the door.
'Will I see you later?' she asked, her words running frantically from her lips.
'Perhaps. I will let you know,' I said. I may as well have stabbed her in the heart. The affect was the same.
'Don't do this to me, Robert. Don't go again,' she said, the tears were welling up now. It was hard to love her when she was like this.
'You do it to yourself, Roberta,' I replied.

I turned to face her, quickly kissed her cheek (body contact is important in moments like this) and I was gone. I would leave her for two months this time or maybe I would only come back when the masterpiece was complete and her essence was ready. These performances made me tire of her. This latest encounter should be enough for her to finish her novel now and for me to finish her.

25. London - Present day brothel and Italy 1546

For a whore house the ceilings and walls were very decorative. There was something dramatic, if amateurish, in the crudely drawn people and places that graced the room. I lay on my back watching as the smoke from my cigarette polluted the common majesty (a paradox) of the room. No smoking was allowed of course but I was not subject to the rules of humans. I had my own set of rules.

One of my Masters, one of my male one night stands, knew how to paint ceilings and walls. Go to Italy today and you will still see his work gracing the buildings that his body once walked in. His death is, of course, 'unspecified'. My work again, my being greedy.

I took him under his religious paintings. What a thrill it was, to commit sodomy in front of the painted eyes of so many saints. They looked on with their shocked eyes even though churches are very familiar with sodomy in my experience. He wept of course after the act. He was not crying because of the act, he was crying because of where it had taken place, in religious surroundings.

I laughed for days afterwards. I would say to him 'You waste your talent on religious matters for there are no Gods.' He would whisper in reply, 'I let the devil have me.' The devil being me. When I took his essence he saw it as confirmation that I was Satan but I am not Satan. I am me. I am not a hypocrite like he was. Despite having a wife and offspring he had formed many 'attachments' with men, some even of noble standing.

Ha, nobility, the word really does not suit the people who it is named for. Because I took him in front of his religious paintings I was the devil but the various other men who took him away from the prying eyes of painted Gods were respectable. Like I said, he was a hypocrite. He was amazing also. His work was epic, his brush a magic wand. The rush from his essence was one of the strongest ones I had experienced to that date and I happily swallowed it all down. I was a better me then. More ruthless, more lost in my 'cause'. Over the centuries I have become more aware of the consequences of my actions and I hate myself for this personal decline, though you would probably see it as an improvement on my character.

I have no idea why I am reminded of him in this present day whore house after sleeping with a rather rough looking woman. She has no grace. She has damaged teeth and a damaged mind and is too old for the game and yet she still takes part in it. I pushed her face away from mine. I did not want to look at it. She was a hole, and a well used one at that.

He was beautiful and talented, sensual but always full of guilt. That was why I only took him once. A week later I took him completely. Some records say he died of a fever. I can tell you that he died of shock. In that moment, in his death, he knew that I was right, that there is no God. For if there is a God how can there be me? Where am I mentioned in the Bible? I am the essence eater of Masters who can travel through time like he owns it. Where is my place in heaven and on earth? He knew, when I took him, that he had dedicated his life to nothing. That realisation would kill you. It has killed me many times yet, unlike him, I live to tell the tale.

26. California - 1984

Sometimes I have taken a Master's essence and fate has stepped in and killed them, relieving me of the job. Once they are dead, the essence is no good to me. I have to take it while the blood flows through their creative veins. The pineal gland of a corpse means little to me.

Sometimes I sense when my Master is in danger and just before the danger hits them, I swoop in and take their gland and allow circumstances to do the rest of the work.

One of my Masters had a volatile relationship with his father and I knew that this would be the death of him.

The 1980s was a strange decade for me to be in. I had my share of Masters but few were created in that decade. Their genius had materialised in the sixties and seventies and had come home to roost in the 80s.

This Master had helped shape the sound of music in the 1960s but it was his smile that I found so memorable. Men who smile the way that he did do not deserve violent ends but such is your life. Violence does not discriminate. It will penetrate anybody, anywhere. It will find a way where there is none.

This Master had ended his life as he had begun it. There was a history of violence within his family. What is it about the strict, religious father that makes him turn to his belt time and again to discipline his offspring? Why does religion always have to have a brutal, physical answer to everything? Would a word of advice, a sentence of nurturing not be just as effective?

My Master never found out the answer to this as his father just beat him time and again. He beat that beautiful singing toddler until he could cry no more. The Master carried on singing though. Singing saved him, that and the loving presence of his mother. For every wound that the father inflicted, the mother tended. For every stern word that the father screamed, the mother whispered gentle words of encouragement.

My Master fantasised about being a pilot. I would laugh as he pretended that his chair was the cockpit and that he was flying to exotic destinations. He found the reality of being a pilot a poor experience and soon abandoned the idea. Why fly when your voice can soar? His chosen path had been decided when he was born but who was I to interrupt his play time to tell him what he really should be doing with his life? He already had one cruel ruler in his house in the shape of his father. Why should I add to the masculine negative atmosphere?

Like all of my Masters I flitted in and out of his life watching as he formed quartets and failed miserably at making his mark on the musical landscape. Even the Masters must fight the demon of failure in the early days. One day everything fell into place though and he found himself revered and loved by many. With that love is money to spend and jealousy from that lifestyle.

Sometimes if I lie down and really concentrate I can hear his last words to his mother so clearly, even though it was decades ago. He was fighting for her right up until his father took his life. I knew what the father was doing as my Master tended to his mother, soothing her. I simply knelt next to him and started to draw the pineal gland from him. He stopped talking, started to grab at his neck. He thought at first his father had hit him around the back of the head but his father's assault was to come.

As I crashed to the floor with the rush of the Master's pineal gland I heard fireworks going off in the room. At first I looked up towards the ceiling, expecting pretty colours and shapes to be filling the air. The only colour to be found was red, as it rushed from my Master's body. He slumped near to me and I rolled away from him and as far up against the wall as possible.

I stared at him as he fought for his life. His eyes widened. Did he see me? I smiled and lay on my back. I let his essence take me to so many places as I drowned out the activity in the room. All around me were screams and movement but I closed my mind to them. I had his essence and I had not had to kill him for it. His father had done my dirty work for me and this made the moment so much more pleasurable. I felt indestructible in that moment.

27. London - Present Day

I feel weak. I cannot lift my head from the pillow. It is as if the blood has drained from my body. Even breathing is exhausting. I lay there for a while, assessing myself like a doctor would his patient. My legs feel cold, as do my feet but it is not cold outside. I have that strange cold about me. I am spiritually cold. Yes, my condition is not physical, it is spiritual. I am shattered. The situation with Roberta has become intolerable. I do not know if there is a way back into her heart. I have tested her patience too much.

I was suffering from a peculiar illness. Was this love? I needed to see her but I could not bear to see her. What if she rejected me?

I managed to drag myself from the bed and made my way to the bathroom. I turned the light on and looked in the mirror. I looked awful. Dark circles had claimed my eye area. My skin was pale. I looked like a junkie near the end of his life and that was what I was.

I was not sure if it was Roberta or just the natural progression of things, but I could sense no other Masters at present. It was as if I had lost my sixth sense for them.

The worst part was I did not overly care. If I was to die now, in this god forsaken century then so be it.

I turned the light off and crawled back to my bed and lay on it. I stared at the ceiling and grimaced at its lack of originality. They did not make ceilings like they used to. They made nothing like they used to. Houses, cars, music, people. Everything was monotonous and boring. This was my illness. I was allergic to the 21st century.

I turned on my side and let out a groan. I was in pain. It was only October. I still had a couple of months before I needed to eat again. I should be at this stage in the last few weeks and not now. Was I dying after all? Maybe my life was coming to an end, with or without an essence, and I had found nothing out about me. I would 'die' never knowing what or who I am.

I closed my eyes and I tried to visualise a good time, a time when Masters were in abundance and I did not care how or when I took them. Where had all the Masters gone? Were there others like me? Were they killing them all? Or had somebody pulled the plug on the pool of creativity and it was all draining away?

I needed Roberta. I needed to see her. I had to see her. I would see her.

28. Spain - 1989

Some Masters are more eccentric than others. Some let the material world consume them despite creating such wonderful masterpieces. One of my Masters loved excess and luxury and all it had to offer. He was born one May morning in 1904 close to the French border in Catalonia. His birth came 9 months after the death of his brother's.

If you believe in reincarnation you may entertain the nonsense that his brother was born again through him. I have no place in my mind for such notions. Unfortunately the Master's parents believed in this and even took my Master to his brother's grave when he was five years old to tell him that he was his brother reincarnated. I was standing at the grave when they told him, shaking my head in dismay. I wanted to materialise then and grab my Master by the hand and say 'Shun that nonsense' but I had to let him be exposed to the childhood that his parents saw fit.

This reincarnation theory stayed with him throughout his life and he often compared himself to his dead brother as though they were two drops of water but with different reflections. I liked that comparison. He placed his dead brother in so many of his later works. He needed his brother's image as much as he needed water to survive.

His father was strict, a lover of discipline, a middle class lawyer. His mother was her husband's opposite. I can only be grateful for this for had she not showered the Master with indulgence and fantasy he may not have given birth to his own form of creativity. Perhaps that is an unfair statement for his father would put on exhibitions of his son's work. He was not completely detached from the Master's creative endeavours.

I watched as the Master grew from a confused five year old boy into a man with long hair, sideburns and elaborate clothes. He had so many admirers that poets gave their hearts to him willingly. He was often too consumed by painting to entertain matters of the heart. I watched, amused, as he rebelled against conformity, always causing unrest wherever he went. He flitted in and out of Paris to meet fellow artists who he loved. I have feasted on a few of them myself. I spent so much time in the city of love, observing him, falling in and out of a false love with him myself.

As his love life blossomed, bedding women too old for him already attached to others, his relationship with his father started to crumble. The Master's father eventually threw him out of the family home and threatened disinheritance. It was all so dramatic for me to watch for I love to watch life's tragedies being played out before my eyes. Life is a constant free play or film for me.

Of course over time his father forgave and forgot. Time wears the human down eventually until you humans forget what you were ever angry about. Or perhaps you choose to forget because what else is there to do, if you are to move on with your life, except to give yourself amnesia?

So many decades I spent with this Master watching him flourish and flounder in equal measure. He was near perfection to me except for his love of Catholicism. He would renounce it and return to it over and again. This caused me great irritation. I excused his religious laziness for the civil wars and world wars that he lived through. Conflict on a global scale can make humans question their purpose on earth and whether or not there is more to the violence, blood and unrest in the every day. When he was indulging in religion, I stayed away from him. There were other Masters to stalk and feed upon.

I cannot recount his whole life to you. It would take too long. I laughed so much at his antics though. He used to border on the childish in his dress and temperament but he was addictive to watch. His life was one long publicity stunt. There are too many creative mediums to discuss regarding him. There are too many moments of genius to cover to do him justice now. Do I need to tell you how high I got off his pineal gland? I thought I would die from the ecstasy of it. I think I love Paris and New York so much because he did, and as he gave me so much pleasure I associate these feelings with those two places.

I watched as the love, that nearly cost him his relationship with his father, started to dissolve. His wife was placed in an ivory tower and even though it was his possession he could not visit the tower without her permission. This detachment from his significant other weighed heavily on his heart and affected his health and his gift. It was even rumoured that she was poisoning him and that this poisoning had affected his nervous system and in turn his creative output. It was me though, always stretching out to take his pineal gland and almost touching it. Then he would do something wonderful again and I would decide that I would not consume him that day.

He thought that my presence was that of his dead

brother's. He would call out, 'Brother, are you still a droplet of water? I am not a droplet of water. I no longer want or need water. I need you.'

After his estranged wife died he denied himself water. He said it was for art and yet I knew that he wanted to die and that was why I decided not to take him. The art was drying up but he did not want to live. I wanted to take his life when he wanted to live. Sometimes I thought that he sensed what I wanted, he sensed my presence. Once he said to the air, 'You cannot have me. Your chance is gone,' and proceeded to set fire to the room he was in. It only made me admire him more. I watched as the flames danced around his defiant, unusual features. I wanted to applaud him for he was a living piece of art. Why did the Master have to create art when he was art?

He escaped the fire and I let him go on for another four years before taking him. It was the 1980s, the decade that had so few current Masters. I believe that was why I let him live for so long even though his creative work had all but dried up. It was like I knew that the decades would get leaner and so I needed to cling to the Masters born in the early part of the century. I had to store them up like you would store meat in a freezer.

His heart gave up as I appeared before him. He detested me for he was expecting his brother or the God that he had entertained so much through his life.

He was too weak to fight me though. I took him and that act itself was enough to kill him. I did not need to do anything else and I was glad of that for I did not wish to deface him, to mark him.

As I fell into a chair, my body in the state that an essence normally put me in, I managed to tilt my head to the side to look at him on the bed. He was so still, just like a painting. I had silenced a living symphony orchestra of a man. The only sound to be heard was the dripping of a tap. Droplets of water were hitting the surface as I allowed his essence to assault me again and again.

29. London - present Day

'What has happened to you?' Roberta asked as I fell into her arms just like my favourite Master had fallen into somebody else's arms once. I had knocked on her door but not said a thing. The cockiness was gone. The confidence had been washed away. It was as if she sensed it. I was a wounded creature. This was not the time for battle. This was the time for understanding and healing. Her anger for me started to dissolve as she helped me to her couch. I sat on it in an awkward fashion as if sitting for the first time and not sure where to put my arms and legs. I could not look her in the eye at present. I could not.

'You need a doctor.'
'No, please. I do not. I just feel a bit sick.

‘You look like you’re dying,’ she said. Her voice was genuinely concerned. This pleased me though I was not sure why.

‘I am not...dying. I just need something to drink.’

‘What can I get you?’

'Water,' I said. It pained me to look into her eyes. I could see the hurt that I had caused her living there.

Why was she making me care? Or did my present weak condition leave me susceptible to these weak feelings? I watched her as she left me to get my drink. A lifetime seemed to pass as I awaited her re-entry into the room. She handed me the glass and I managed to sip from it. I felt the water running down my throat and finding a home within my insides.

‘I would forgive you if it had poison in it,’ I said and now I found the strength to look straight into her eyes, unflinching.

I could see tears desperately fighting not to come out. Her mouth was strained as if she did not know what expression to hold on to. In the end a faint smile escaped but only lasted for a moment.

‘I can only say sorry for my behaviour.’ I took another sip of water. She said nothing as there was nothing to say. It was an unsatisfactory response to the anguish that she had felt at my hands.

‘You need a doctor,’ she said again. I shook my head.

‘I don’t understand you,’ she decided and went to walk

away from me.
'Roberta, wait. May I stay here tonight?'

My question hurt her heart but she did not show it. She went to speak and then changed her mind. She was trying to read my face, to understand my motivation for this unexpected appearance.

'On the couch...of course,' I added as if it needed to be said. Her face suggested that I would never enter her bed again with her permission.
'You may but it would be good if you were gone in the morning.'
'As you will have it,' I said. The spontaneous, act of compassion was being replaced by the boredom of formality. How could I stop this rot? How could I make her see my pain as well as her own?
'One more thing, Roberta,' I said. She humoured me by nodding her head.
'How is your writing going?'

'Fine,' she replied slightly suspicious. It was more than fine. I knew that her novel was almost perfection. There were just a few alterations needed and it would be the ultimate dress of her achievement to wear forever.

'I am happy for you. Perhaps you will let me read it one day.'

Her face seemed distant, cold. I was not winning her over. I had caused too much damage perhaps. Was there any point in putting the scaffolding up to try to repair us? Perhaps a demolition was in order. It was one or the other. I would not allow us to decay naturally. Whatever became of us would be at my hands, no other.

'Perhaps,' she said with no conviction. There was no lasting stare, no hope to be found in her expression. She left me in the room, sitting alone in contemplation. Her behaviour had taken my mind of my physical condition and this was one positive to cling to.

I placed the glass down and managed to turn my body into a lying position on the couch. Each move felt false, restrained. Rigor mortis seemed to be setting in on me even though I still breathed. I feared to close my eyes in case I did not wake. Did I even want to wake? What had she done to me? I had swallowed the murders. I had come to terms as best I could with my aimless killing days. The look in her eyes had made my heart weak. I despised myself for it.

30. London - Present day and a memory in the form of a dream

The bar smells peculiar. I cannot quite put my finger on the smell. Is it death? Is it food left out in the open for too long? Is it a mixture of blood and sweat? Whatever it is I find it distracting as I make my way to the bar to get a drink. I am not sure of the year. I want to say the 1980s. Yes the clothes and the hairstyles suggest this decade but I cannot put my life on it. I will not put my life on it.

'Vodka, straight, no ice,' I say to the barman who nods his head, approving of my no thrills drink. It makes his life easier.

I watch him as he turns from me to place the glass against the optic. He has a beautiful physique. I can see this even through his crisp white shirt. He has strong hands. I watch as he thrusts the glass against the mouth of the optic to allow the alcohol to flow. Perhaps I will have him, see how my night goes.

'One for me, lover,' a coarse voice asks, too close to my ear. I do not turn to attach the voice to a face. It is unimportant.

'One what?' I ask, still staring at the barman who is now at the till, running my order through.

'I was thinking vodka but whatever you want,' the voice said. No dignity to be found, not worthy of my response.

The barman returns and places the drink down.

'One for you,' I say to him and he smiles.

'I'm fine, thanks,' he says, taking my held out note.

'Are you sure?' I smile back.

'I'm sure,' he replies and walks off.

'I said I'd have one as you're offering,' the unwelcome voice says again.

'Fuck off,' I say in a gentle voice, almost barely there

voice. I do not want to waste my energy on it but I want them to hear my words of disdain all the same.

'I know your kind,' the voice says. I do not respond. I drink the vodka instead.

'I know what you are,' the voice continues. My eyes remain staring ahead, looking into the mirror placed behind the bar.

'I know what you feed on,' it says. This time the choice of words interest me. I do not turn to face the voice but I digest the knowledge it boasts of having. I want to ask the voice what it thinks I feed on but decide to play the silent game for a little longer.

'I know your kind,' it said again.

'You know nothing,' I decided.

'I know what you hunt down, why you're here in this bar on your own.' The voice was now dangerously close to my ear. I wanted to swat it like a fly but thought better of it. There was more narrative to come and I wanted to hear it.

'You're looking for people like you. You're looking for what I am.' The breath gently blew on my neck but it was not a pleasant sensation. It was not erotic by any stretch of the imagination. I felt disgusted by it.

'I saw how you looked at him. The way you looked at his neck. You're hungry for him,' it continued.

I signalled for the bartender and pointed at the vodka optic. No words were necessary. He knew what I wanted, drinks wise.

'Are you going to buy me a drink this time?' the voice

said, more slighted than angry. I said nothing as I watched the beautiful barman carry out his duty for my pleasure.
'We are alike. You have found another like you. Let me in,' the voice said.

I paid the barman and turned to face the voice. A man is attached to it. He is in his twenties, ravaged by life, good looks ruined by the demon that is alcohol and drugs. It becomes all too obvious at once that he is a gay prostitute. He believes me to be gay, hunting men just like him. While I have had many men, and could be considered a prostitute, I am not here for them. I am looking for my kind, the killing kind, the eater of Masters.

At first his words gave me slight hope that I may have come into contact with one of them, despite his lack of social grace. Anybody was better than nobody to share this burden with.

I gave him a smile, downed my vodka and abandoned the stool.

'Leaving? Got a bit too real for you?' the voice said. I grabbed his arm as gently and discreetly as I could.
'I hope that it does not get too real for you,' I whispered and then left the bar.

That is where it should have ended. I should have left

him with those words but I was so angry with him. I was angry that for a fleeting second he gave me hope where there was none. You're looking for people like you. You're looking for what I am. That tiny bit of hope was like a firing squad as I fell against the wall outside the pub, clutching at my chest as the night air assaulted me. I was enraged, I was beyond rationality. I tried to calm my breathing, I tried to let his words flow out of my body and into the night but they remained like buried bullets.

To my shame, I hid like a thief in the darkness, a stealer of life. I waited for him to leave the bar and I followed him for a while. I mimicked his footsteps and his movements. I watched as he staggered through the park in the darkness and I fell on him.

'I will show you my kind,' I whispered and proceeded to break his neck like it was a stick. I kicked his lifeless frame away from me and started to stumble away. I managed to get a safe distance from the body and then I fell. I thought I would fall through the earth but I did not.

'I will show you my kind,' I wept into nothingness. My life was dedicated to taking creative Masters but now and again I took a life through rage or passion. I had no idea why this memory decided to surface as a dream, at this time, but it did.

As I lay on Roberta's couch, invisible tears started to

fall. I was so alone, so want of recognition in another. Perhaps Roberta's rejection had triggered the memory for though she was not my kind she was the closest I had ever felt to a meeting of minds, a meeting of something. I was in pain but the bluntness of her behaviour tonight was by far the worst blow I had ever suffered. I eventually fell asleep with the vision of her eyes and the words 'I will show you my kind' in my head.

31. London - Present day.

'What kind?' Roberta asked me as she sat next to me on the couch. I could tell by her body language that she was still angry with me but her curiosity was the greater emotion at present.
'What kind?' I repeated with a false confused face. I had obviously been talking in my sleep. 'You kept saying I will show you my kind. What kind?'
'I am not sure. I was probably having weird dreams.'
'You look a bit better than yesterday but you could not look worse than you did.'
'I think somewhere in there is a compliment.' I immediately regretted the words. They made her frown. It came out like I was trying my luck with her, too soon, and after her allowing me to stay.
'You should go and see a doctor,' she said and stood

up.

'I do not need to see a doctor.'

'Well I have a busy day ahead of me so I don't want to ask you to leave but-'

'-say no more. I shall go,' I said, getting to my feet.

My legs were not as unsteady as they had been the previous day. She was right. There was a slight improvement. Perhaps just being around her was the reason for my feeling a bit better.

'Will you be ok?' she asked. She was walking at a safe distance behind me as I made my way to the door.

'I will be fine,' I said. I would have to be. I turned to face her. One last dramatic gesture before leaving, hoping my words and actions may win her around.

'I would like to say sorry again for my behaviour. You are a good person and you did not deserve it.' She nodded her head in response but no words came.

'I hope to see your book one day, gracing the shelves. I shall buy a copy. I shall read it,' I decided. She said nothing. She did not even nod her head this time.

'Do you not think that portmanteau is the most beautiful word in existence and that suitcase will never be a sufficient word to replace it?' I said.

She looked confused by my question. I wanted any expression other than the cold one that she had given to me. Confusion was much better to remember her by. My hand opened the lock and pulled back the door.

'I think that most words have been replaced by words

that are not sufficient but even the more elegant words could never be enough to describe you.'

This was my parting sentence to her. I did not look back to see its effect. I just kept walking. I walked to the end of the hall, into the lift, out into the lobby and out of the building. I would never walk out of her life though.

32. France - 1948

I was back in Paris, the city of love. It was not just the city of love though. It was a city of tragedy also. So many tragedies caused by love in one way or another. Love was killing me just like it had killed so many others.

I digress. It is March 4th and I have come to consume a Master who has been told that he is dying. I am not going to let him die of a disease such as cancer. I refuse to watch his body decay like fresh fruit left out to rot. I will be taking him with purpose. I do not need to consume, at present, there is no need except for the need to ensure that he does not die a slow painful death.

His parents were Greek but he was born in France. He never lost his fascination with his Greek ancestry though. He was one of nine children but only two survived. He lived, of course, and a sister. He nearly died when he was four but remained on this earth. For somebody who suffered so much in life, life seemed to want him to live. For what? Did life just see him as a toy like a cat sees a mouse?

The childhood illness played havoc with his immune system and as a result it left him a nervous and fretful child. The child became a man and the nerves got worse. 'Worse' is not an appropriate word really. He spent his whole life suffering from depression and returned to mental institutions like a boomerang. Like so many Masters before him, a constant battle with the mind led to such creativity.

I watched as he pursued a career in writing, the theatre and the cinema. He was involved in so many disciplines. He directed, he produced, he philosophised but he also declined so much. Declining mentally was his true gift. I often observed him as he put strange thoughts to the back of his head and tried so hard to be 'normal'. These periods of 'normality' did not last for long. I did not need to tease or torment him like I had other Masters for he did a splendid job himself. His philosophy regarding theatre performances was both ground breaking and completely absurd all at once.

I travelled with him to Mexico after some failed productions he had indulged in. I travelled all over with him really. He loved to absorb himself into different cultures and different people. I knew why. I had spent many years observing him in good and poor mental health. He did not understand who he was or where he had come from and so instead he tried to understand others and their place in life. I could see so much of myself in him.

I watched him suffer the effects of heroin and escape from the clutches of it. What a pair of junkies we were. What a junkie I still am. And then came the true decline. He had many mental battles but none as bad as in 1937 when I feared for him. I, who had seen so much. Two years before world war two he was fighting a battle to stay sane that has never been rivalled in my opinion. The soldiers of the brain are determined and they will fight how they want to and not how we want them to.

The cycle of life became hotel trips that he could not pay for, deportations and being forcibly removed from properties. Material items reject the rejected in a way that nothing else does. If you are insane, you cannot survive in the world of business and money. Sanity pays the bills though sometimes I wonder on that.

He was labelled an 'undesirable alien' and what was worse was that he did not seem to care about this label though it kept me awake at night. My Master was far from an undesirable. I desired him greatly and if he was an alien for seeing things differently then so be it.

He spent a lot of time in straightjackets. I would hover near him and he would laugh in my direction as if he could see me. He probably could in his own weird way. I should have taken him at that stage but he was still thinking so much. As long as a Master thought, I did not like to take them. Thoughts give birth to masterpieces. I needed masterpieces like you need oxygen. Do you understand?

He spent his final years in asylums, all of the time. The good days did not come back again but the thoughts remained and so did he. Of course there was a bigger madness spreading throughout France by then. Nazi occupation. The Nazis were never made to wear straightjackets though. They wore smart uniforms with perfectly polished shoes. Insanity dressed up to the nines while my Master remained restrained in filth for free thinking. Your world is insane.

And then came the electric shock therapy. It was the stuff of nightmares and caused much controversy. I often held his hand as he endured it, though I am not sure that he felt it. He was one of the few Masters who I could not fully work out for he was cavorting with insanity like it was going out of fashion. Still, the controversial treatment made him pick up the pen again and start writing. Who was I to deny him that?

So many names were given to my Master to describe his condition. Schizophrenia became almost as a familiar word as my Master's name. Sane people always feel that they have to name and box things. 'Heaven' help you if you get out of the box. My Master saw the world how he wanted to. Where was the tragedy in that? Bound, shocked, left destitute for not thinking like others and I wonder why there is a shortage of Masters today. The human race has had creativity and original thought beaten out of it.

Now I was with him, as he sat alone, dying of cancer after a lifetime of pain. The war had been over for three years but it was just starting for my Master. How many battles had his body and mind thrown at him on a daily basis? This was the battle to end the war though. Was there anything so formidable an opponent as cancer?

I sat next to him as he lay on the bed and materialised before him.

'I have come for you,' I smiled.

'Are you St Patrick? Do you want your stick back?' he asked me. I shook my head.

'No, there are no Saints, there is only you.' I smiled and he smiled back at me.

Wars, terminal illnesses, vile treatments and yet he died smiling. He saw death as a gift and I was happy to give it to him.

33. London - Present day

I had lost my gift. I had to conclude this. I could not 'sniff' out a Master, like before.

I had taken to reading the newspapers, keeping track of 'celebrity' columns though most people were celebrated today for doing nothing. None of these pineal glands would suffice. I had dined on innovators and creative storm chasers. How could I possibly lower myself to eat the essences of lesser genius types? I was an addict with principles. I had feasted on the best. My head hurt. I pressed my hand against it. I was aching for something, for someone.

I abandoned the bench that I had been sitting on and made my way to a local cafe. These were the kind of haunts that potential Masters frequented. This is where the likes of my Roberta were. My Roberta, except she did not appear to be now at all. I did not believe that I had completely lost her but I did believe that she was slowly disappearing from my wretched life.

I ordered a black coffee and sat at an outside table though the weather was quite uninviting. The tail end of autumn was never a serene affair. Everything was dying. As the leaves lay discarded on the floor, the wind whipped them up into a frenzied dance and carried them away from my view.

I loved autumn though. It was the one season where life and death truly were bedfellows.

I stared at the people sitting outside the café. There were few for the weather had dictated that the inside of the establishment was the place to consume beverages today. I was looking, searching for a Master. Inside the cafe there were students nursing small cups of coffee that had not been refilled for the past hour. They just wanted somewhere to sit out of the miserable weather that was not their dormitory. There were mothers drinking hot chocolate and allowing their children to taste it. There were no Masters.

My breathing felt laboured, restricted, though I had recovered a bit from that night with Roberta. I was not fully well but I was well enough to sit and watch the world go by with this cup of coffee in my hand.

'Penny for them?' a voice said. I looked up to find a gentleman smiling at me slightly amused by my expression. I took an immediate disliking to him though I could not say for sure why. He was handsome with a beautiful voice and yet his eyes unnerved me. I did not respond.

'Ah, you wish for more than a penny for them?' he decided. He sat next to me, without asking, and placed the gloves, that he had removed, onto the table.

'For what?' I asked.

'Come, come. Everybody has heard of that saying. Why even a babe in arms or an aged person rotting in a seaside retirement home knows it.' He continued to smile at me even though I did not return it. This annoyed me all the more.

'What are you drinking?' he asked. He was too brash. He had no manners. Did he not understand that my behaviour meant that he was not wanted at this table? This was a time for reflection, not interaction. Still I answered him.

'Black coffee.' The two words fell from my mouth and hit the floor with a thud. Even my words were lethargic. I was too exhausted for a conversation with this grinning stranger.

'An excellent choice. I shall get us another two coffees and we shall drink them together and watch this world go by.'

Before I could respond to his proposal he had left me sitting there and had entered the cafe. I stared at the gloves on the table and then looked towards the cafe windows to see where the man was. He was at the counter, probably ordering coffees as he said he would. His confidence was a source for my irritability.

For some time I just stared at his gloves and then I felt compelled to pick one up and assess it. It appeared to be leather. I smelt it. It was.

'Slink, of course, made from the skin of unborn calves. That is why they feel so soft. You want to try them on do you not? You are welcome to,' he said, as he placed our coffees on the table. I placed the glove back down.

'The skin of the unborn? How nice of you not to let them experience life so that you can have soft gloves,' I said.

I was annoyed at myself for saying it but he had pushed me to it with his overbearing ways. Who did he think he was? Who did I think I was? Speaking like a man with morals when I killed for pleasure. I was a hypocrite of the highest order after all it would seem.

'Yes, I guess it would be better to let them experience the joys of life and then brutally take them away from it.' He smiled at me as he said this. I could tell by his eyes that there was so much more that he wanted to say but his words would remain limited for now.

'You appear slightly at a loss, if you do not mind me saying. Only disintegrated love can make a man want to sit alone and drink coffee on a cold, metal seat in a social surrounding,' he said to me. I watched as he placed two sugar cubes into his cup.

'I do mind you saying actually.' I went to stand but something made me want to stay sitting. He was a vision. He intrigued me with his soft gloves and his intuitive ways.

'I am sorry then,' he said. He sipped his drink and stared at me like I was a lifelong friend. He was too familiar with me for my liking. I knew nothing of him but I felt sure that he had my soul in his hands.

'Do you like this cafe?' he asked. It was small talk to relieve the tension that had built up so rapidly between us. I welcomed it for I did not want to leave but I was not sure how long I could stay in his company.

'I have never been to this one before actually,' I said. I decided to join him by drinking the coffee that he had bought for me.

'Me neither. Is it not strange how we should both decide on this day to drink here?'

'I think you give too much credence to it. There are

many cafes throughout London and oh so many people.'

'Yes, many people but not many like you,' he said.

He placed his cup down and smiled again. I could not work out if the smile was mocking me or was sincere. It curled a little bit too much at the edges for me. I decided there and then that my original thoughts on this man were correct. I did not like him. I no longer wanted to be in his company.

'Thank you for the coffee,' I said. I stood up to leave.

'Going so soon? Just when I thought we were getting along so swimmingly,' he said and joined me by standing up. He picked up his gloves and placed them on his hands. I do not know why but I had to watch him. I was drawn to him.

'Perhaps I could walk with you?' he said.

'You do not know where I am going to.'

'That does not matter. I care only to walk and I do not mind in which direction,' he said.

'I would rather walk on my own,' I said and bowed my head at him.

I had never bowed my head before but I was hoping that this would be seen as a final, formal gesture. I wanted him to understand that I was walking away on my own.

'Yes, of course. You have always walked alone. I will see you on the path again though,' he said with that smile again. He bowed his head and then proceeded to walk the other way.

In that moment I did not see myself in him. I did not see my kind and yet I was inexplicably drawn to him.

34. London - 1912

I have taken so many Masters from Ireland you know? I have drunk so many pints of Guinness and downed so many Irish essences. I have got drunk on the country's hospitality as well as their creative children. I have no idea how the emerald isle became the butt of jokes in common conversation for that place has given birth to genius time and time again.

One of my Masters from there created a character that reminded me of myself so much. A character who could defy time, living off something other than food.

He was the third of seven children and I watched as he remained bedridden until the age of seven. I was not at his birth. I did not sense his genius then. It was when he was about five years old that I sensed his creativity. It was about 1852, and I was drinking and whoring and somewhere in between those two activities, his name came to my head.

I can remember placing my drink down and just walking. I walked for what seemed like a life time but in reality, it was a moment. I found myself back in Dublin, I had been before and I certainly returned a few years later for another Master.

I hovered at the window, staring in at him. He was five years old and bed ridden with no obvious explanation. I believe that the mother had Munchausen by proxy syndrome and I do not care much for what you think of that theory. I maintain that. How can you be confined to a bed for seven years and then miraculously recover and go on to even be an athlete? No, she kept him there, somehow, in that bed.

Maybe she sensed me as a mother? Maybe she thought that if she shielded him from life he would not have anything to write about? She was completely wrong. His bedridden days gave birth to all kinds of ideas. Instead of running and grazing his knees, like most children, he was running around in his head and marking his mind. His thoughts would come back much, much later and the pen would follow.

It did not help that she filled his mind with tales of superstition and the supernatural as no other could. The Irish need their tales of the supernatural as much as they do the air that they breathe.

I watched as he became interested in theatre, even becoming a critic but this was not his calling. I was waiting for that one particular novel that I knew would make him the Master who I craved.

I sighed as I watched him marry. It was a mistake, in my eyes, though she was a beauty. By now you will know my opinion on Masters forming relationships and if you do not know have you been truly reading this story?

Be alone and create forever should be the code of Masters however this Master and wife had a successful union. She had been desired by another Master of mine but she chose the current Master that I speak off. It is strange. Often my Masters cross paths in their lives. Some are just acquaintances. Some become dear friends looking out for the other. How strange that I have consumed friends. They knew each other in life, and they knew me in death.

I went to Whitby with the Master in 1890. I had to be there for I knew this visit would be the spark that would create the formidable character that would live forever on book shelves. I could hardly miss it. I was fond of Whitby also. I had been there so many times before. There is something quite beautiful and melancholy about English seaside resorts do you not think? I have seen them in so many states of progress and decline and yet something remains. Unlike footprints that dissolve when the sea water runs over them, the magic and energy of the seaside remains.

It was not just the seaside that inspired him though. There were the ragged stones of Scotland, crypts and European folk tales that he digested. Whitby was like the match that lit the fire.

I digress. I travelled with him to Whitby, watched as he

did the mundane things like unpack. Of course he wrote novels before and after 'the' one, but I did not take him. Once again I cannot explain why I did not take him when he completed the masterpiece novel for that was why I had started following him in the first place.

I just kept watching him. Observing as he juggled a theatre career with his writing. The original masterpiece manuscript was lost of course and found again in the decade that at times I would rather forget; the 1980's. I find it amusing sometimes that the manuscript re-entered the literary arena in that god forsaken time scale. He had hidden it from the world. I think that he sensed my coming and felt that if he hid the original physical representation of his masterpiece that I would somehow forget that he was a Master. I never forget my prey.

He died five days after the sinking of the Titanic. He had had several strokes and nobody could really conclude why he died. Some say syphilis, some say overwork. It was me of course. I was hungry, I wanted him. After all this time I wanted him. I think I held back at first because he had created a character that I could relate to. His character was a man, not quite a man, hovering in the shadows of society, waiting for his kill to sustain his life. The Master had created a character that could not die the way that mortals did and so I drank the character down. It felt wrong to take the father of that invented character for he made me feel like there was somebody else out there like me, even if that somebody was fictional.

35. London - Present day

I reminisce more and more about my past Masters now I find myself in a drought in this decade, your century. I also find myself focussing on the past more for I cannot communicate with Roberta. She had made it clear from our last meeting that she did not desire my company at present. I was still checking in on her, observing her and making sure that she was coping. I used to spy on her to ensure that she was finishing her masterpiece. Now I just wanted to make sure that she was happy. My absence did not appear to have the same effect on her as it had in the past. Sometimes I felt that she was missing me and at other times I thought that she could hardly remember me.

'Reminiscing again?' the voice asked and I recognised it immediately. It was him, the stranger with the soft gloves.

He sat on the bench next to me, without my permission of course. He did not need to ask for permission. He had a face that said 'I rule the world'. I wished that he would exit mine.

'I reminisce often myself for there is so much to reminisce about and so little in this life time to appreciate. I am sure that you would agree,' he said.

'I am sure that I have no idea what you are talking about,' I said, hating the fact that I had responded yet again to his questions but hating myself so much more for knowing that he was right.

'I am sure that you know exactly what I am talking about. These are lean times. Whatever happened to original thought I wonder?' he said. I cannot explain it but his voice was almost hypnotic, entering my ears and searching for what was left of my spirit within.

'There is no such thing as original thought.' The words fell from my mouth against my will.

I silently cursed myself. He let out a gentle laugh in response. This angered me though I remained calm. I must not let him see that he gets to me. That he crawls under my skin and sets up camp within my marrow, veins and bones.

'Winter will be upon us soon,' he said. I looked up to the sky, as if expecting snow to fall.
'I love winter. It is death in season form and there is nothing so vivid and life affirming than death.'
'That makes no sense,' I replied, too quickly. He was grinning; I did not need to look at him to know this.
'What has sense got to do with the seasons or the inevitability of death, my friend?'

I looked across the field at the trees shedding their clothes. The sky was threatening rain. I looked everywhere but at him.

'You want my company but you are not sure why,' he said. His voice was like music from the past, vague notes playing until they started to sound familiar.

'You flatter yourself,' I said as nonchalantly as possible for I was burning up. My heart was quickening. I wanted to stand and rip my shirt from my body and scream for the rain to fall. He did this to me, somehow.

He sighed and tapped his stick against the floor.

'You really do not know who you are but then do any of us?' he said. He found his feet, he was hovering over me like a black cloud, threatening.

'I know who I am,' I lied, still avoiding his eyes.

'You have no idea who you are but this is not a tragedy. Weep for the man who knows himself. Where is the fun in that? Nothing left to discover? Nothing left to realise.' His voice was filled with certainty. I had the feeling that he knew what I was. What I am still. He was intoxicating and yet I must remain sober to him.

'She has no idea who she is either but you know...and I know. Such is this weird life. Everybody knows everybody else but nobody knows themselves.' His voice seemed to be fading with every letter.

'You speak in riddles,' I concluded but when I looked up, he was gone.

36. Florida - 1969

It was a beautiful autumn morning. I do not believe I had ever seen such a sky in all the centuries I had walked the earth as I saw on that day in the dying months of the sixties.

My chosen Master must have felt the same for he was sitting near the window consuming the view and his favourite whisky and malt liquor. In between staring at the sky he was writing notes for an idea for another book. I was never going to let him complete that though. He had become too engaged with alcohol and I worried for my essence. I feared that if I allowed him to go on drinking the way that he was I would miss my opportunity. That he would drink himself to death before I could take him.

I hovered before him as quietly as I could. He had no idea that I was in his presence. This was probably due to the intoxicated state that he was already in so early in the morning. Yet even in this state, he was still trying to write. He was phenomenal.

I placed my hand near to the skin of his neck and started to draw the gland from him. I was excited and turned on by the idea of eating his essence for he was responsible for stream of consciousness writing styles so I knew the hit would be sublime.

It was in my hand and I stared at it as he dropped his whisky glass to the floor. He felt sick. He grabbed at his stomach and then he ran for the bathroom, vomiting blood as he moved as quickly as he could. It would appear that I would not need to do a thing. I could enjoy this creative tablet without worrying about the aftermath.

I sat in his favourite chair and allowed the essence to assault my senses. I wanted the view of that sky as feelings of bliss enveloped my body. I was such a sophisticated junkie.

I saw his life, as always, playing out for me. He was such a stern child but with such devotion for his mother. Too much some may say for he compared all women to her and found them wanting. I saw his brother dying in childhood and the young Master clinging to his mother for comfort. His mother had sought comfort in false Gods while his father had turned to manmade houses of gods such as gambling rooms to forget.

I could see Catholicism and athleticism filling up the time line of his life. I witnessed the Navy near turning him mad. Who would it not turn mad? Then the words that he had created over time started to appear for me, in front of my eyes. There were gold letters floating all around my head as I started to come down from the effects of his pineal gland.

I was shocked back into the chair and could hear activity all around me. There were the cries of a screaming woman and flashing lights. My Master was being rushed to hospital. Blood was all around me. He could not stop vomiting it up.

I picked up the glass that the Master had dropped and poured a whisky into it. I walked over to the window and looked out for that sky. It had darkened all of a sudden, lost some of its colour. This pained me somewhat for I do so love a beautiful sky. I drank the whisky down and placed the glass back on the floor where it had originally fallen.

The Master died the next day. Nobody could save him. They blamed alcohol, they blamed past medical conditions. They blamed everything and everyone bar me. I was the blameless one and yet I was the cause of it all. As another decade was dying away, I realised that I was just like a decade. I took everything with me and I left everything behind and somehow it was not my fault.

37. London - Present day

I awoke in a sweat. I left the bed and went into the bathroom to pour a glass of water. I was in a hotel with a stranger. I had fucked one stranger, with all the strength that I had left in me, to get the other stranger out of my mind.

I looked at my reflection. What was looking back at

me? I did not know. I had never known. I did not want to know, I think, now as I write this. I swallowed the water and felt it sliding down my throat.

In the dimly lit bathroom, two hands came behind me and started to stroke my chest. I placed the glass down and leaned back into the darkness. The hands, in such a predictable fashion, were now searching for lowers parts of my body, rubbing the area gently, whispering words in my ear.

I turned to face the body and spun them around and pushed them against the bathroom sink in a rough fashion.

'You whore,' I screamed as I fucked at the body, pulling at the hair, biting into the neck. As we moved in and out of the light I caught sight of the face. It was the stranger with the soft gloves, smiling, moaning. I forced myself into him harder. He was crying out in ecstasy begging me for more. I went as deep as my body would allow. Then in another light it was my Roberta. I slowed my pace, became gentle with the rhythm. I stroked her face, she moaned with begging eyes. Then it was the whore from the bar that I had picked up. I brutally finished the action and I pulled out and pushed her to the floor.

'Get out of my fucking sight before I break your neck,' I said, almost breathless.

She gathered herself up from the cold floor and ran

back into the bedroom. I heard movement in the room. Clothes being picked up, personal items going into pockets and then the door slammed.

I smiled at myself in the mirror. I was not sure why. I went back into the bedroom and lay on the bed. It was now obvious to me that I wanted the stranger. I wanted him sexually and in other ways that I had not quite worked out yet.

I was aroused but also tearful. I lay on my back and looked up at the predictable, banal ceiling. My mind was joining my body, it was decaying.

38. Mexico - 1954

One of my Masters knew all about the body decaying. Her body had tormented her throughout her life. Was it any wonder that she hoped never to return to this life?

She was not born a Master. Some are. I have discussed this before. Some I have to be at the births for and then there are some like her. Circumstances made her a Master. She had an interest but it took an accident for her to unleash the genius inside of her.

I came to her after the accident that nearly killed her. It was violent and horrific and yet she made beauty come from it. It left her immobilised for months and robbed her of the right to motherhood but she gave birth in other ways. She constantly delivered thought provoking art work that could outlive any children that she may have given birth too.

She was in incredible pain on a daily basis but she did not complain. I would sit at the edge of her bed and watch her as she started to paint whatever was near to her to take her mind of her injuries. She did not care what the surface was as long as she could paint it.

After her confinement she was never quite the same but she had a new friend. Art. Art would be her saviour if nobody else would. Love could not save her. Once again, she should not have married and certainly not the man who she had chosen but some Masters will follow the path of matrimony and I must let them. Life experiences shape the Master and I must not interfere even when things turn violent and undesirable. Her marriage was a vivid and destructive mistake and one that she made twice. It encouraged her to paint though and I cared so much more for the talent than the person back then.

Despite nearly dying as a child (so many of my other Masters nearly exited life in their early years) she went on to be a strong, independent woman who would not allow her weak body to define her. I was of course sexually attracted to her. I did not make the mistake that I have made in present day though. I kept my distance and did not make myself known to her. She did not need me to 'inspire' her when her own body and partner did that on a daily basis with the misery that they caused her.

Her wretched life made her produce hundreds of paintings. Her work was inspired by life and not what life could be. She danced when she could, she smoked and she played with her sexuality. She did all of this as if sticking two fingers up at the world that did not seem to want her in it. I loved watching as she had sexual encounters with women. I wanted to join them as they pleasured each other but had to keep my distance. I knew that when I consumed her I would consume these moments also and would be rewarded with the most wonderful climax. She should have only let women in really. She had always been too much for a man. Perhaps that was why I chose to remain hidden from her. I was after all in the male form.

When her female form could be cut no more and when she had endured all that she could I came for her. It was what she had desired. She had said so in her diary a few days previously. She wanted constant death and I could give her that. I offered no afterlife. I only offered an eternity of nothingness.

The strong woman who had dabbled in politics amongst other things was now ready to allow death to assault her. She was not afraid for what could be more frightening than the life that she had been given? The only thing of beauty to come out of her terrible existence was her work and she did not need to live for it to survive.

She was frail as I approached the bed. She had suffered from too many ailments over the years for one person to cope with. I still feel that she sensed me as I approached her for her eyes seemed to start to shine as I stood over her. I did not say anything. I just leant down and kissed her mouth. It was not a sexual kiss. It was an act of admiration. I had flitted in and out of her life and watched as her physical form attacked her again and again and her mind had remained strong. Her mind had remained strong enough to create the body of work that she was leaving behind. It was a remarkable achievement and she deserved nothing but my respect.

I cannot share with you the final moments now for I feel sad as I recount this. I need to preserve the moment and bury it. I have the same feeling that I have about Egyptian tombs being plundered and exposed to the world via museums. Some things should not be put on display or discussed. Some things are sacred. Her last moments are for me and her alone.

39. London - Present day

A week or so passed by. I was not sure how to measure time any longer. I seemed to be losing my faculties. All I knew was that I needed to see Roberta and I needed to see the stranger even more. He haunted my dreams. He came to me with cryptic messages and then he would kiss me, his tongue searching for answers that I did not have. Every time a dream passed, I thought that I understood him a little more. I was connecting more with his words, his ways. How could I hate him when he was so like me? Was he just like me? Was he whatever I was?

I had to see him again. I yearned to fall upon him.

I went to the cafe where we had spoken. I sat on the bench that we had sat on. I frequented all of the parks and cafes of London for him over time and then he found me.

'I must speak to you,' I said when he approached me. He smiled. Roles had been reversed. He sat next to me without asking. This time he knew that he did not have to ask for I wanted him to sit next to me more than anything. I stared at him. He opened the newspaper he was carrying and started to read it.

'Please, I must talk to you.' I hated myself for this. Begging was not my thing. I was all powerful, all seeing. He had brought me to my knees in two meetings and I would gladly stay there for him.

'Now you want to speak to me?' He said the words in that wonderful voice, laced with enough wisdom to fill the sands of time. I had to stop myself from leaning in to kiss him. I wanted him desperately. He folded the newspaper and placed it on the bench between us. Was this a barricade? I did not know. It made me want him more.

'And so, my friend, what is so urgent that you would walk the streets of London for me?'

Was it just a question or did he know that I had been doing just that?

'I need to speak to you in private,' I said. I sounded pathetic, like the women who I had laughed at, their desperation grating on my nerves.

'There is nothing that needs to be said in private. There are things to be done in private but there is nothing to be said,' he whispered into my ear. I went hard at his words, at his breath on my ear. I could not find words. What was he doing to me? I felt something touching my ear, wet. I realised it was his tongue. He was licking my ear.

I pulled away in shock. We were in public, in a park. He laughed.

'It is 21st century London, my friend,' he said.

I stood up and started to move away from him. I did not want to but I was the strong one. I did not like this change of circumstances.

'Follow me,' he said and started to walk away. He knew that I would follow him. I ached for him. I needed him.

He led me down an alleyway. It was deserted. I looked

at him confused. He pushed me against the wall and roughly grabbed at parts of my body and then he started laughing. I was mortified.

His expression changed. He looked on me like I was an insect.

'You were so easy to break. I am almost disappointed. I thought you would be more challenging.' His words cut into me. I had said it so many times to others. To have them thrown back at you was more painful than imaginable and yet I could not feel pity for myself.

I leaned against the wall still fighting for breath.

'I have watched you for so long and I thought it would take forever to break you. You are worse than her. She is human, you are not,' he said. His words terrified me. He did know what I was. He leaned against me and gently grabbed at my throat.

'Of course I know what you are. I am not here for you though. I have come for her. You are right. She is the only Master worth taking this decade. I have kept you distracted while she has happily written away. She is so close now and then I will taste her.'

He let go off my throat. I could not move. I was paralysed from the information. He was my kind. I was not unique. How many others? There were so many questions and yet I could not find the words.

'Why?' I managed to ask. I was starting to feel degraded. I was starting to understand how others had felt at my hands.

'Because I can,' he said with a smile.
'She is not yours to take,' I said. The words angered him. He squeezed at my throat again.
'Oh yes she is and so are you. I will be coming for you again. That you can be sure of,' he said.

He walked away. I felt my body sliding to the floor. I had hoped for so long to meet one of my kind but not like this. All of the centuries of hope flooded away as it dawned on me that I had been used, just like I had used others. He had made me want him; he had all but taken me and would take what was mine. There was something much worse than this though. I still wanted him. I needed to warn Roberta.

40. London - 1707

Love can kill. Love can torment. I never quite understood the strength that love can exhibit until my dilemma with Roberta Downs. One of my Masters was so overcome by rejection in love that instead of inspiring him it made him simply want to exit life.

Sometimes I go to weddings and I sit in pulpits trying to understand that sacred union. I cannot. I have often heard his music ringing out though, threatening the stained glass windows, rising above the altar and then out of the doors and into the open air.

How could a man who was responsible for a piece of music associated with love, end his life in such a miserable, lonely way?

I was with him when he was thinking of the various ways to take his life when it became clear that his chosen woman did not want to be part of his. Should he hang himself? Should he let the water have him? He would let a coin decide only the coin insisted that he live for it would not land on a side but embedded itself in mud, tilting at an angle. He so wanted to die though.

He is one of my kills who I never feel guilty about. I stared at his saddened face as the coin refused to land on a side of choice. I knew that I could have him then.

I am not fond of guns as a way of suicide but sometimes a situation commands one. As he sat in the grounds of the cathedral trying to want to join existence again I crept up behind him and begun my essence stealing act.

He did not even feel my presence. He was numb to everything but her. I almost felt bad for it was so easy to steal from him all that made him who he was. I did not need to reassure him or explain why I needed him.

With the essence in my hand, I took the gun from my pocket and shot him in the head. He fell to one side and the familiar colour of blood began to run from him.

I lay down and looked up at the sky and allowed the process to take over my body. His most famous piece sounded like a thunder storm as it invaded my being and enveloped me. It got louder and louder as my body began to climax. I thought that the fantasy sound would rob me of my hearing but it slowly started to turn the volume down as I came down from his pineal gland.

I hated taking the lives of musicians and composers but if they wanted to die was I not just being kind and considerate in ending their days and aiding my survival? Before the stranger came I used to ache to speak to somebody about my feelings regarding my kills. Now I wished for my unique existence again where the stranger was not a threat to Roberta and words were not necessary.

41. London - Present day

'I must speak to you, Roberta,' I was shouting through the door. She was ignoring me and understandably so. I knew, even more now, that the way that I had treated her was unforgiveable.

'Please let me in. It is urgent,' I said. There was no movement from inside. She had tired of my coming and going. Perhaps he had already visited her? I could walk through this door myself. It was not a barrier but she could not see me do this. I had to remain human, vulnerable to her.

'This is not about us. This is about you,' I said. I waited. Nothing. What was there to do but to leave for now and respect her wishes? I would try again tomorrow.

I started to walk away. The door opened. She was standing there, looking beautiful and composed. She must have finished the masterpiece and yet I did not sense it but then I was not myself. I had weakened so much.

'Say what you have to say here,' she said.
'I would rather say it inside.'
'Then you will not say it at all,' she said. She went to close the door. I put my foot there. Not violently just in a preventive fashion.
'I will speak here,' I said. She paused, as if considering and then she opened up the door again, releasing my foot.

'There is so much to say to you. I would like to apologise for my behaviour. I was, I am a terrible person.' I waited for a response. None came. She just stared at me with cold eyes but was there warmth behind them? I had to believe it.

'I have never felt for anybody the way I feel for you and it got too much. I got confused. I had to distance myself from you,' I said. Surely this would provoke some kind of reaction? The words seemed to anger her more.

'Please do not finish your book,' I said. This was the sentence that got a response. I could almost see the anger boiling inside of her.
'Why?' she asked.

What to say now? There is a being, like me, who lives on the pineal glands of Masters and if you complete your book he will feed on you? Just like I had planned to until something changed in me? Yes, looking at her now, I knew that I could never go through with it. I could not take her like I had taken her mother. I could not. I would not. I had to protect her.

'Well?' she asked, getting ready to close the door again. There was only one way to stop her and it was to hurt her but then do we not always hurt the ones that we love?

'Because I lied to you...you cannot write. You do not have a talent like your mother did. You have her money but you do not have her words,' I said. I could feel the vowels and consonants stabbing every part of her body. She was wincing with pain. She held the door for support.

'And?' she said, fighting back the tears. I hated myself but not as much as I would hate myself if he had her. She was mine to claim, not his.

'You will be a laughing stock and stain your mother's good name in literary circles,' I said. It was the final verbal knife and I flung it with as much force as possible. It hit her in the chest. She closed the door on me.

'Think of your father,' I said through the door. 'He does not want a daughter for a writer,' I added. I could hear her breathing on the other side of the door. My false words were confirming her worst fears. That she was a failure. That she would never live up to her mother's reputation. She was destined, like me, to walk in the shadows also.

'I love you,' I said to the door. They were three pointless words.

I came through the wall to see what my verbal assault had done.

She was sitting against the door, staring into space. The tears were falling though she could not feel them. I hovered near her. I wanted to lean down and kiss her. I wanted to pick her up and tell her it was all lies and that she was a genius but I could not let him have her. I went to stroke her face and thought better of it.

'Mum,' she said, sensing somebody there. Her mother was bones. She was not here to comfort her. I had made sure of it.

42. Kent - 1882

The Kent seaside air is inviting as I make my way to the resting place of my chosen Master. The April air is cold and unforgiving as each of my steps takes me closer to the grave where his bones will live for eternity. I think I have already told you that I love the English seaside. I love the smell in the air, the sound of the sea dominating the area.

A few more steps and I find myself in the graveyard where his gravestone calls out to me, his murderer. The place is empty as I approach his last home, mortality trapped under stone.

I lean down to look at the inscription which will, of course, fade over time and be unintelligible to future mourners and curious passer-by's. I placed a single rose on his grave and sighed.

'Well, my friend, how do you find death?' I asked the air as I stood back up, erect.

I looked around and took in the atmosphere. Some people found graveyards comforting, peaceful places. I found them sad and regretful. I had filled so many over time.

This Master was already dead when I killed him. He was housebound, a consequence of his consistent drug addiction and penchant for whisky. Many things changed throughout his life. His women, his beliefs, his work were all susceptible to the ebb and flow of life's river but his terrible habits? They were the only permanent part of his life and they were his undoing. He fixated too much on women and religion at times also and these contributed to his mental decline when he tried to portray his feelings through poetry. Why write when you can paint like the stars have fallen from the sky and landed on your canvass?

His relationship with religion caused me such disdain. Like any of my other Masters I avoided him when he was lost in false Gods. I soaked up his pain when his 'beloved' wife died though. I all but bathed in his suffering as he lowered her into the ground and buried her with some of his written work.

When I took him he was still trying to complete his depiction of a prostitute. It amused me that his legacy built on portraying religion should end with an incomplete painting of a common tart. But then prostitution is rife in religion for pious men must make whores or saints of the fairer sex. There can be no in between.

I picked up a stone and threw it across the graveyard. It landed with a 'thud' on top of a grave with an elaborate headstone.

'Damn this earth. Damn your God. I am your God. I am your taker of life. When you have become worm meat I will be still flesh and bone and fucking the images of the women who you so tirelessly tried to paint,' I said to his gravestone. What could he have said in reply if I had said it to his face while he was still alive? He could not deny it. I was executioner. I was life's Master.

43. London - Present day

I wished to be in another century, another time, when Masters were in abundance and my conscience did not irritate me the way that it does today. Another week had passed by. So many hours wasted with me wasting away. I was unsure of myself and what to do.

I stood over Roberta, like a freak of a guardian angel, her saviour and yet the cause of all of her problems also. I had killed her mother. I had destroyed her childhood. What can I do? Shall I let this play out? My words had backfired on me. It had made her even more determined to complete her work. How could I stop her? Only the truth would stop her but it was so unbelievable and worse, if she did believe it, she would hate me.

This was how it felt to have no control then. How I differ from the narrator from the start. Why did I care? Let the stranger have her. Let me not eat and see what happens next. Why not choose inactivity for once?

'She is so close. Can you feel it?' the voice came. I was horrified that he had found his way into her home.

Perhaps he had always been there, choosing now to show himself.

'Ha, perhaps you cannot. You are weak. She will taste amazing I am sure.' He placed his hand near her hair and pretended to stroke it. I winced at the display of false affection. Her hair was not his to stroke.

'Come closer so I can lick your ear,' he laughed. I thought I was a monstrosity. He made me seem docile. How had I not sensed him over the centuries? Had he always been here watching and waiting for me? I could no longer remember if I had felt him or not. My present condition made me unsure of so much.

'Are you falling out of love with me?' he said. He was by my side so quickly. I flinched at his presence.

'See how she writes for us? You are so weak though. You can barely stand. How will you defend her against my advances?'

I ignored his questions. I concentrated on standing by her side, ignoring the desire to fall to my knees. I knew I was weak. I knew that time was running out. I had come to peace with this. I just had to protect her from him and then I could 'die' peacefully.

'You cannot keep her safe forever. You will fade away if you do not eat and as you will not eat her you will fade away for sure. I will claim her then. I have many months on you. I am guessing that you last had something to eat in the winter gone. You are as close to fading as she is to completing,' he tormented me. I felt helpless but I stood still like a resilient soldier, fighting on a losing side.

There was a knock at the door. It woke Roberta up for she had fallen asleep at her desk for a while. I liked to watch her sleep. If she was sleeping she was not writing. It was her father.

'I need to talk to you, Roberta,' he said. She let him in with slight hesitation.

'I have a gift for you,' he said. His manner seemed different, as if a weight had been lifted from his shoulders.

'I have been speaking to Susan and there are things that I need to get off my chest,' he explained.

He sat next to her on the sofa and handed her a bag. In it was a picture of the sea in a photo frame.

'It was your mother's. She used to have it on her desk to inspire her to write,' he said. Roberta ran her finger along the image and smiled.

'She imagined a place by the sea for us where we would live happily ever after. She thought her writing could buy us that paradise,' he said. Roberta was still smiling.

'Thank you dad,' she eventually said and hugged him. 'I shall place it on my desk.'

'I have only ever wanted to protect you. Paradise became...hell in the end,' Clarke said. Roberta touched his face.

'Not quite. She left us but we did not leave each other. We are still here,' Roberta said. Clarke nodded his head.
'And I intend to be around for a long time,' she said.
He wanted to say so much to her. He was frightened of what writing would do to his daughter. He did not want her to be driven mad by it like her mother was but he had to take it slowly. He had made progress. He had brought Willow back into their lives with a picture. She did not have to be the dirty secret that could not be discussed, not today.

'Have a tea,' Roberta said. She stood up and placed the photo frame on the desk.
'But you are busy?' Clarke said, looking at the computer.
'I need a break. I was asleep before you came,' Roberta smiled. Clarke returned it.

I looked to the stranger. He grimaced at the display of affection and disappeared. I lingered, like the unforgiving spy that I am. My breathing was laboured, my movements painful but my mouth smiling.

44. Wiltshire - 1930

Everybody should get the chance to live until thirty at least in life do you not think? Three decades is not asking for the world is it? Thirty years to create some memories to take into the afterlife if there is one? Three decades to make some bonds that, when they are severed on your death, cause indescribable anguish to those left behind?

I have no idea why I took him that summer. I did not need to. I was not desperate for an essence and yet I had him. I watched him train as a painter in Paris. I watched him drink and exchange ideas with the greats such as succulent Picasso. I travelled to North Africa with him in the 1920s, trying to understand what he was searching for as his feet walked on alien soil.

He was like me. He was confused about his sexuality. He was a beautiful, bright thing and that was perhaps why I took him too soon? He had so much more to produce but when I stared at him sometimes I wanted to break his neck like I broke the necks of strangers in moments of madness.

I think, looking back and writing this now, that I wanted him sexually and his exploits angered me. I hated his older, gambling lover who was coarse and uninteresting. Every time he lay with him, I pulled my hair out in rage. A man of his talent and beauty should never allow a lesser to defile them but he did time and time again.

The sound of a train can sometimes bring him to the surface of my mind. It has now as I travel through London, not going anywhere in particular. I just love the sound and movement of this form of transport though it has changed so much over time. I take a train journey whenever I can and just stare out of the window, observing your ever changing planet.

He was a drug addict. Opium was his choice of decay. He became so paranoid by life and his own work that he started to carry a gun in his pocket and this was the beginning of the end for him. I often feared that he would pull the trigger and destroy his brain before I had a chance to unpick it so I had to step in too soon. I think I had to take him? Do you understand?

I had followed him to a restaurant and allowed him one more meal with his sister and mother. I had allowed him to discuss his latest work, his hope of future exhibitions. I had to let his family have this moment with him so that they could cling to it in his death. Perhaps, even then, I was not all that bad a creature.

As he stood on the platform awaiting his train, I reached in and took his gland. He was one of the few Masters I have taken in public. It was spontaneous. Something told me that he was going to end his life by jumping in front of his train so I just took him.

He started to feel dizzy. He started to step dangerously close to the edge as the train pulled in and so I just gave him a gentle push. As I heard his body making contact with the train, I fell on the platform floor and rolled into a corner to allow my essence enhancing session to commence uninterrupted.

I did not care for his broken body. I only cared for his beautiful thoughts.

45. London - present day

I have feasted on so many words, notes and paintings but nothing made me feel as full as seeing the damage of Clarke's and Roberta's relationship, caused by me, being slowly repaired. I think I could have weeks to live and die happy knowing one wrong was righted in my pointless existence.

The stranger flitted in and out of the proceedings of those last days as Roberta edited and edited again and I fought a battle to stay alive. Now and again there would be a day of remission, where I could feel myself slowly returning. Colour was coming back into my skin and my heart was beating at a normal rate. My memories seemed vivid and my actions more defined.

As I watched over my Roberta I realised that my mission had changed regarding her. At first she was my chosen prey, my essence for the year. I had willed her on to complete her masterpiece so that I could have her. I had done this by spurning her in love, knowing that my absence would fire creativity in her like it had with so many Masters over time.

Now I had to replace that cruelness with another. I had to make her love me again and I would return it this time, for as long as I had. Nothing doused the flames of creativity more than surrendering to love and all that it had to offer. Contentment would satisfy her enough and then she would put the pen down. He could not have her then. I would protect her.

'Look at you. What happened to you?' the stranger asked. He was disgusted by my unexpected transformation and it sickened him as much as it confused him.

'I do not need to answer to you,' I managed to reply. I was sitting, watching Roberta asleep on the couch. She had tired herself out from her latest editing frenzy. The good thing was she was a perfectionist and where many people would have completed the book by now, she was still not happy with it. This bought me more time and, more importantly, her more time.

'You know you cannot protect her forever, lover boy,' he teased. He knelt down next to her and placed his hand above her face.

'She will complete. I will have her. I know what you are thinking. You are thinking that if you fall in love with her and her with you, she will stop. She will abandon the Master in her and become the little housewife. Have you really thought it through though?' the stranger asked, getting up from his knees.

I said nothing. I watched as he walked towards me.

'You see, there is a problem with your plan. The problem is you. You can make her stop writing for now and delay the inevitable. What do you think will happen when you fall in love, briefly, and then you 'die'?'

'I will not die,' I said. I was angry with myself for responding to the wretch but I had to say it out loud to believe it.

'Of course you will, my friend, and then what? Let me tell you.' He stood behind me and placed his hand on my shoulder. I felt the weight of centuries through his gloves as he pressed his hand gently against my body.

'When you die, she will sink into the greatest depression ever. Her mother gone. The love of her life gone. You know as well as I do what happens under those circumstances.' He let go off my shoulder and walked around to face me. He was smiling in a mocking fashion for he knew only too well that I knew what happened in those circumstances. Magnificent masterpieces were created from that kind of misery.

'And the gland? Ah, the gland. What a prize. I can almost taste it. Better to let her finish it now and then I will race you for it. It is the kinder thing to do in the long run.'

'The kinder thing to do?' I managed to ask. I left my chair so that I was standing face to face with him.

Something in my eyes must have unnerved him for he stepped back slightly as if under attack.

'Why have you come now? Who are you? Why are you here?' I asked, searching his face for the truth for I felt I would not hear it from his mouth.

'I have come now because I sensed your weakness. I am you, my friend. I am here because I wanted to meet you before you come to an end and I must say it is rather disappointing.' I ignored the jibe.

'Are there others like us?' My curiosity was stronger than my anger for him. I so wanted there to be more of us so that before I passed I could bathe in their unity, feel part of something.

He laughed and shook his head.

'My dear man, I do not know. I have not met any of 'us' on my travels. You are the nearest thing to me.'

'We are nothing alike,' I said.

'Come, come, you know that is not true. We are one and the same.'

'No, we are not.'

'What? You are better than me because you developed a conscious several centuries later? You are a hypocrite. You kill, just like me, for your own benefit. Look in the mirror and see you,' he said.

I knew that he was right. I was no better than him. I had waited so long to meet another like me. I had wasted several lifetimes of hope. Meeting somebody like me had made me realise just what I was, a cold killer, nothing more or less. I had tried to act grand and give credence to my unworthy existence and he had verified the truth for me. It was hard to accept.

'I shall tell her what I am and what will happen if she completes the book. Then she will not fall in love with me and she will also not complete the book because of fear,' I said.

I sat back down. It drained me to stand.

'Ha, she will not believe it.'
'She has to.'
'And will you tell her that you killed her mother also?'

'If it makes her stop, yes, I will tell her that also.' It frightened me to commit to that sentence but I would do anything to save Roberta and if it meant the terrible past coming out then so be it.

46. France - 1900

Sometimes I think of him, when the dark comes too soon, when the sky turns the deepest black after being the deepest blue, too quickly. The sky should change gradually; prepare us for its transformation. Autumn throws the sky at us in such a coarse fashion. He died in November, the last day in November actually. I thought he might last till Christmas but life had battered him beyond all hope.

I could not have him. I do not think I have discussed with you just how much it hurts not to be able to have a Master because life takes them. For you mortals, it is like aching for another and watching them in the arms of somebody who is not you. On the last day in November every year I get a dull ache in my heart. I know it is for him and the fact that I did not consume him.

I should have consumed him in 1890 but I did not. 1895 begged me to take him as did 1898 but I held back. His life was so painful, so full of anguish that I secretly hoped that an even bigger masterpiece would be born from his suffering. What a terrible individual I am and as I write this I am glad that he did not die at my hands. I did not deserve him.

He was born in the autumn as well as exiting the world in that season. Fitting, I think. He was born in 1854 in Dublin, a year before the Dublin fair was stopped and many years after the victims of the great famine had poured into the city.

A man born into such a vibrant yet aggressive and suffering population was never going to be ordinary. He was always going to be flamboyant and a stranger to the everyday. He was born to intellectuals and so of course, was fluent in other languages and became a whore of university life. He let education fuck the life out of him. He was a tart for mind expansion.

He left Dublin for London, continuing to allow life to assault him and I was always there. Watching as he allowed feelings for both sexes to develop the way that I allowed it to also. We were so alike. I would watch him as he slept and so many times I wished to reveal myself to him but I did not. I remained watching and studying as he went from experience to experience.

When he completed his only novel, I should have taken him then but I did not. I cannot say why so please do not press me on this. The moment has gone now so it would be pointless trying to revisit it and understand it.

And then, much later came the dark time and that was when the true regret settled in that I had not taken him. To recall seeing him caged like an animal, and yet still creating, hurts my heart now. Had I killed him before he was subjected to sexual rumours and their consequences, I would have spared him incarceration.

I spent so many hours in that cell with him, watching him as he wrote and wrote again. Had he not pen or paper I think that he would have cut his hands and written with his blood on the floor and walls. He had to write you see? It is what made him who he was. Beneath the scathing humour and the wit lay a sensitive soul who was driven by his need to express.

When his sister died something inside of him broke and he wrote such beautiful words to remember her and to dull his pain. Even now when I walk on snow I tread carefully in honour of him, her and his work.

And I watched him marry and commit the same mistakes that so many other Masters did. How I hate love. I hate the union of two people. We should all walk this world on our own. People get in the way. They make us make bad decisions. They stunt our intellectual growth. People ruin everything. Love is like acid. It corrodes everything that has meaning because it believes that it is the only thing that has true meaning.

My head hurts. It always hurts when I think of him and especially at times like this. So much regret. I should have taken him after the one and only novel that he created. I should have swept in and taken his essence and killed him in an imaginative way.

Instead I left him to the rats of society. I let a beautiful soul be marked by ugly hands through misjudgement. I thought he had so much more in him. I thought that he could make it, that he would keep creating.

Instead he died in poverty, away from his birthplace, after decades of suffering and humiliation. I should have put him down. I should put myself down.

47. London - Present day

I needed to see Roberta. Time was running out, I was weakening and she was growing stronger in her talent. I had written her a note in the hope of seeing her. I had asked her to meet me at the cafe where we first met. I had composed the note so many times and then ripped it up. I could not find the words to explain my urgency in needing to see her. I was not expecting her to come but I went anyway in the vain hope that she would meet me.

'I am here,' her voice said.

I dared not look up from my cup for fear that it was a figment of my imagination. I needed to see her though to confirm her presence.

My eyes set upon her face. It was worse than I feared for she did not look angry or pained. She had the face of somebody who no longer cared. What could be worse than nonchalance in intimate relationships? I had been guilty of it myself. It felt strange being on the receiving end of it.

'Thank you for coming,' I said. My voice was weak; I spoke in a low tone.

'The weak act will not work on me this time,' she said and found a seat.

I ignored her comment for I was too busy trying to work out how to say what I had to say. I could feel her eyes burning into me, studying me as though I was a species that should be wiped out before it has a chance to live. It was unsettling.

'It is cold, do you not think?' I said. It was an empty question to delay what had to be said and she, quite rightly, treated it as such.

'Come come, Robert. We are way past weather talk. It is beneath us,' she said. Her eyes were glistening with a triumphant glow. The tables had turned and any other saying that you could think of to comment on this moment. How had I lost my confident, ruthless way? Was it love that had made me this pathetic creature, weak in mind and body?

'You are right. I have not brought you here to discuss the weather,' I said.

'What is it then?' she asked, impatient words from an impatient mouth. Who could blame her? I had treated her appallingly. It was what I deserved. I was surprised that she had even turned up. Her presence gave me some hope. I had no speech prepared as I was not expecting an audience.

'It is hard to explain...' I began and then stopped. It was not hard, it was impossible. How could I tell her the true nature of myself and what I was? She would despise me for it.

'Try,' she said. I knew in my heart that she already despised me so what was there to lose? Yet she did not despise me enough to leave me waiting here for her. She had still come to me, after all that I had done. Was this also love or was it stupidity? Is this what it is to be human?

'There are things in this life that are beyond our understanding.' I said.

'Try me,' she said. She unravelled her scarf from around her neck and it freed her beautiful hair. I watched as the strands fell into place. She was by far the most beautiful work of art I had seen through the centuries and I had defaced her. I was despicable.

'I am not what you think I am,' I said. I looked down at my cup, seeking refuge from her eyes.
'What, you're not a selfish bastard who gets a kick out of hurting vulnerable women?' she said.
'No, I am that. I am a selfish bastard but you are far from vulnerable, Roberta.' This seemed to anger her.
'Don't even start with that. Don't try to assess me. We are here to discuss you, not me. Are we not? If not, I do not care to stay.' She began to stand.
'No, please,' I begged. She stayed sitting.
'There are things that...roam this earth that are not human,' I said.

She looked at me with slight surprise. She was not sure what conversation she was expecting to have but this was not it.

'These things seem quite invincible. They walk among humans and they can talk, laugh, dance, eat and drink but they are not human.' I paused to look at the people in the cafe. Was I talking too loud? I lowered my voice slightly. 'They can have sex and appear to be romantic and kind but they are not human.'

'What are you talking about? I thought we were here to discuss you,' she said. I gave her my most sincere look.

'We are discussing me.'

'So you're not human?' she said, her voice sounded so irate. I nodded my head.

'You are human?' she asked. I shook my head.

'For Christ's sake, just tell me what the fuck is going on. What are you?'

'Not for his sake, for your sake, I will tell you,' I decided.

This annoyed her for she went to stand up again. I grabbed her hand.

'Wait. Give me five minutes and then I shall be gone forever, if you so wish.'

'Five minutes. From now,' she said. Had she a stopwatch she would have pressed its' button. I could not reach her with flowery language. I was irritating her. Her mood would only welcome blunt, short sentences. This was not a time for dramatics. I looked at the people in front of me and to the back of me and to the side of me. I lowered my voice again.

'I am not human. I am not sure what I am. I do not know where I came from. I have lived centuries.'

She had the look of a woman waiting for the punch line. There was none to be had.

'I can live like a human but I can also make myself invisible to people and my life source is not just food and water. I need something else to sustain me, to keep me alive.'

'Oh I see and this other thing? It wouldn't happen to be bullshit would it?'

She stood up. There was no holding her back now. What did I think would happen? That she would just accept my story when I did not truly believe in it myself?

'I am telling you the truth,' I began.

'Do you know how many times I opened and closed my front door before coming here? How many times I talked myself in and out of this meeting? I thought that you should have one more chance, that you may have something sincere to say that would wipe away the weeks of hurt that you have caused. I should have known better.'

She was out in the wintry streets, walking briskly away from me, as far away as possible. I was close behind though.

'Please, wait Roberta. There is so much more I need to say.'

'Oh I bet there is. Screw you. I can't believe I agreed to meet you,' she shouted back at me, her pace quickening.

I was on her now. I grabbed her as gently as I could though she tried to break free from me.

'What if I show you, Roberta?'
'Just let go,' she said in a loud voice. She did not want to scream. She did not want to make an exhibition of herself. She did not like to air her feelings in public.
'I will make myself disappear,' I said.
'Yes, why don't you do that?' She was being sarcastic of course. She broke free from my grip.

I looked around. There were too many people for me to disappear and come back again to prove a point. There were too many witnesses. I had already drawn attention to myself by trying to hold Roberta in my grip against her will.

I watched as she became a dot in the distance. She did not look back once though I willed her to. I would have to do the unthinkable. I would have to enter her home without her permission and show the real me to her. She would have to believe then. She would have to listen to me.

48. New York - 2007

When I came for him his belief system, regarding the supernatural, crumbled all around him. He did not believe that the likes of me existed and yet I stood next to him in his New York home on that day in April as if we were neighbours. He had reached out to touch my face to ensure that I was real. I will never forget the touch of his skin on mine. It sent electricity through me.

I have already discussed the drought that I find myself in regarding Masters. There are so few creative individuals coming through for me to consume. I have evolved though and part of me welcomes this mass exodus of talent for could I feast on them anyway? I believe that my killer instinct is sleeping.

Still in New York in 2007, for no other reason than being in the neighbourhood trying to 'sense' Masters I decided to take him. I did not need to but I wanted him. He was one of the inexcusable kills that I regret. He was in old age, he could have lasted a little longer but my greed got the better of me. I did not need to feast on him. It was spring time.

I wanted the gland of the man who had written one of my favourite books. He was a Master but I did not kill all Masters. I had wanted him to live. I am trying to explain my actions but I guess that I cannot. I must be honest. Sheer greed made me enter his house to take him.

He had survived so much in his time. Wars and personal tragedies were the fabric that made the cover of the bed that he lay in. What could be more tragic than your mother killing herself on Mother's Day? The woman who had carried you and brought you in to this world had decided that she no longer wanted to be in it. How do you endure life after that? Suicide tendencies run in families so I often reassure myself that had I not taken him on that April day, he may still have killed himself.

I watched as he abandoned writing so many times and returned to it again. He despised religion, like myself, and saw it as a disease for the lonely. Towards the end this changed slightly. Old age and the threat of death even started to sway him to believe in false Gods. So many humans turn to God, in the hour of their death, after rejecting him their entire life. He was human as well as a Master. I had to forgive him this.

There were so many mouths to feed in his life also. I would watch him struggle with children, embracing the role to the best of his ability. Should Masters even have children I wonder? The only nurturing they should partake in is that of their work.

I digress. I am in New York on that April morning and the Master had stroked my face. He instinctively knew why I was there. His eyes widened as he realised that my existence had opened up so many new doors to his mind that he will not have time to open. They will remain closed. I will make sure of this.

I was not successful in my essence stealing for one reason alone. Panic. I had chosen to show myself to him at the top of the stairs and so began a fight to the death. He was not going to allow me to just take what I had come for. He was a former soldier of war and a current soldier of his personal life.

As we wrestled at the top of the stairs and I tried desperately to reach in for his gland, he gave me one final look of defiance and flung himself from the top of them. I could only watch as he started to descend in an awkward fashion, getting ever closer to the bottom.

I remember that moment in slow motion as I followed behind him. He had once said that every character should want something. I wanted that gland as his broken body came to rest at the bottom of the stairs.

Then came the anguish. His head had been destroyed like a custard pie dropped from the top of the Empire State Building. I still tried to pull the gland from him as his breathing started to close down but nothing came. It had been destroyed. My desire had ruined everything. He had passed on for nothing.

I remember falling to the floor and lying against him, listening to his last gasps of breath. I told him that I was sorry. I must stop writing for one moment. Please allow me this.

I had wanted him so much for he seemed to understand so much about me through his most famous fictional character. He knew how it felt to cheat time. He had written about it. He knew of loneliness and being misunderstood. I could not ask for his help now like a son to a father. He could not help me understand who I was because I had decided that I needed my drug when I could have absorbed his brain in a different way. I hated myself as I lay there but it does not come close to the hate that I feel for myself now as I type this.

49. London - present day

'It did not go according to plan with lover girl then?' the stranger asked. Though I was sitting in a pub of the beaten track in a dark, dusty corner he still found me. I should say nothing in return but I could not help myself where he was concerned.

'Fuck off,' I decided would be the best sentence to express myself.

He sighed at my words.

'So vulgar. It does not suit you. I do so hate the warring language of this century,' he said as he sat next to me. It was the one thing that we agreed on.

'I believe that I did not invite you to join me,' I said.

'You did not but I do not have to ask your permission, my friend. These seats belong to the world, not to you or me. And to think once you would have loved me to have sat next to you,' he smirked. I detested him. I drank down my whisky.

'Dutch courage?' he asked. I ignored him.

'You were so beautiful and now you are like a fading,

drooping flower,' he said. He pushed a glass of whisky towards me. I had not realised until that moment that he had bought me a drink.

'It is always such a shame to watch a statue crumble. You really will have to eat sooner rather than later,' he said. I stared at the drink. I did not want it for he had bought it for me and yet I needed it. To my shame, I picked the glass up and drank the liquid down.

'That's the spirit, if you will pardon the pun. I like you, and I think that you like me,' he said.
'No, I never liked you,' I replied very quickly. This made him laugh.

'I think you like me. I think that you think that I am beautiful. I think that you may have even wanted me had things not turned out the way that they have.'
'Just go away,' I said.
'Why? There is another scenario for us to embrace here, my friend. You have looked for a companion for so long, over these long, lonely centuries. Here I am. I can be your companion.'

I sniffed at the suggestion. If he was offended his voice did not show it.
'I think we would make a good team. We would not be lonely any longer. We could look after each other and even share our essences.'
'Share?'
'Yes, I was thinking we could have half of Roberta's

essence each. I mean people halve their drugs and I was thinking-'

'-well stop thinking,' I said. I got up slowly, like arthritis was settling in, and slid the whisky glass back to him.

'Did you think that a drink could buy me? I am not that cheap,' I said. He stayed sitting and smiling.

'Not a drink, a bottle perhaps.'

'Not all of the vineyards or distilleries in this world could make me be your partner.'

'Well that is too bad. I was going to share her with you but I am quite happy to take her for myself.'

At his words I leant over with all of my strength and grabbed at his jacket. I was a warrior on the decline. My body betrayed me. I could barely grasp at him. How could I fight him? He knew this.

'You stay away from her,' I whispered. I looked around the pub to see if my display had drawn attention. It had not.

'Or what, my good man? Come, we know that we cannot kill each other. Let us live together, you and I. She is nothing but a human. They are ten a penny. We are decadents, you and I. Lovers of all centuries, living impossible lives outside of morals. Have you forgotten what you are?'

I let go off his jacket. I had not forgotten who I was. That was the problem.

'You were like me not so long ago. Do not look upon me like I am the monster. You are me. You think that you are in love? We cannot love. You know this. Hearts as black as ours do not beat for love. Ours beat for essences. You should accept my offer,' he said.

'Or what? You will kill me?' I mimicked his question.

'No, you will kill yourself.'

'I will take the chance,' I decided.

'She is mine. I am coming for her. I will beat you to her. You know this. Think on it. Do not be a fool. Do not throw away your fabulous past and many futures for a woman,' he said after me.

I did not respond.

Out in the cold streets of London the moon shone on the pavements. It lit up the 21st century way of life with its' discarded litter, condoms and cigarette packets. I closed my mind to it all. Had I had the strength in me I would have broken a stranger's neck for the anger that I held inside. Luckily for passing people I was too weak for such spontaneous cruelty. I was angry because I knew that what he was saying was in part true. I was just like him. I had been just like him. I was angry for falling in love and placing myself in a situation hard to bear. I had always said that love was not worth dying for. I felt helpless. I felt human.

50. London - 1963

So many of my chosen Masters have felt like I do now but none as more as her. Whenever I see bumble bees flying past me or dying in the streets her face comes to my mind. Her father was fascinated by them. He even dedicated books to them. I liked her father for he rejected religion. He died too soon though this was not my work. Her father was not a Master. I had come for his daughter. He died when she was a child and this was one of the contributing factors that would lead to her never quite being able to abhor life though she loved the academic world. I could never kill a bee now for it would be like killing her again.

She was born in the autumn of 1932 in Massachusetts. I was not at her birth for I did not sense then that she was a Master. Life made her a Master and helped her to break down boundaries in poetry.

I watched as she entered the working world finding it undesirable. What she had hoped for in her profession and what materialised were worlds apart. Then the dark days that stole the light from her existence began. I lost count of the times that she slashed at her skin to see if she had the courage to end her days. Then the 'real' suicide attempts began. Taking pills, crawling into dark spaces hoping that death would find her. I was not ready for her though. I knew she would create. I liked to see suffering back then also. I took pleasure in watching human beings break and fall in their worlds.

She was institutionalised for months on end and subjected to regular degrading treatments. Sometimes I would visit her there and sometimes I could not bear it because the treatment was stunting her creativity and I needed her essence.

One day she flew from there like a determined bumble bee and set about making her true mark in the world. She travelled. She met and fell in love with a fellow Master who ended up falling in love with another. Need I comment further on marriage? Her husband liked to keep bees. It is funny how life goes full circle and you humans end up marrying your parents at times.

I could tell that the depression that she had fought so bravely throughout her short life had her by the heart. Her husband had gone. She had two young children who she could not invest in emotionally though she desperately wanted to.

It was so cold that February. She lit anything she could to create fire, including the oven. Nothing seemed to be working properly. Even the plumbing was betraying her. I knew what I had to do next. I knew that her life was coming to an end you see and that pineal gland was sitting on its' throne, ripe for the taking.

So, as she sat crying, in the early hours of that morning I came to her and put my hand on her shoulder. I loved to watch suffering but even I could not bear to witness hers any longer. She placed her head against my hand.

'I am done,' she said.
'I know,' I whispered back.

I gathered some towels and covered the gaps in the doors and the windows. She watched me but she was not really there. She had already left this life. I came back to her and smiled and stood behind her. You know the rest. The old me would love to go into detail about the high I got from her and how I dragged her body to the oven to make it looked like she had gassed herself. The new me is struggling to recall these memories. They are getting shorter and less descriptive. I have become like a bumble bee. My next kill will kill me.

51. London - present day

I lay next to her as she slept. I watched her breathing like a guard on duty. The stranger would not be the reason that she would draw her last breath. She would be an old woman with children and grandchildren surrounding her. She would not be her mother. I had to make her see. I had to make her believe.

The minutes passed as I watched her chest rise and fall. Sometimes her breathing was laboured. She would moan or raise an arm or kick a leg out from under the blanket only to cover it again. I could have watched her sleep for eternity but unlike before, I felt that I was no longer the master of time. Father time had me by the throat and he was choking the life out of me.

The light started to seep in through the curtains. It seemed to affect her eyes for she started to blink slowly. Then she opened those beautiful eyes and saw me. She went to let out a scream but I placed a gentle hand to her mouth.

'Watch,' I said and made myself disappear and reappear. I let go off her mouth and she jumped out of the bed. She started to back away from me.

'Get the fuck out of here now or I'll call the police,' she screamed.

'And say what?' I said. Her reaction was not the one I was expecting.

'Just get out.'

'I will leave but only when I believe that you understand what is happening. I just disappeared in front of you. Does that not frighten you?'

She did not reply.

'Look I need to say-'

'-no, you need to go,' she said. She started walking backwards away from me, like I was a wild animal about to pounce on her. Her eyes were wide with fear though her words and voice suggested otherwise.

'Watch the table behind you,' I warned too late. She almost fell on it but remained composed.

'I turned your computer on that night and I threw your mother's book from the shelf,' I said. She kept walking backwards away from me, stunned.

'Watch the chair,' I said.

The back of her legs made contact with the chair but she did not flinch.

'You called your father because you thought it might be your mum but it was me,' I said, watching her as she made her way to the kitchen. I realised what she was trying to do. She was arming herself with a knife to protect herself from me.

'I would not bother with the knife. You just watched me disappear. I do not think regular weapons are going to be useful,' I advised her.

Still she reached for a knife, a potato one. It was quite comical. I tried not to smile. I knew a smile would confuse and anger her even more.

'Get out, you psycho stalker,' she said. She now held the potato knife in my direction and made a jabbing action with it as she spoke.

'Yes, I can understand why you would conclude that. Did you actually see me disappear though?' I said. I could not believe that it was not having the desired effect. If I was human and saw somebody disappear before my eyes I would have been nothing short of astounded. She was more concerned by the fact that I was in her property without her allowing me entry.

I watched as she ran to the bathroom, knocking

anything out of the way that was in her path. She slammed the door and I heard her lock it.

'Come out of the bathroom,' I said, walking over to the door. She said nothing.

'I can walk through doors, Roberta. How do you think I get into your flat without a key?' I said.

'Just leave, please just go.'

'I am coming through the door now,' I said.

I heard movement behind the door as I walked through the wood and into the bathroom.

She was standing in the bath with the knife close to her chest. She let out a huge scream. I climbed into the bath with her and released the knife from her shaking hand and covered her mouth. I pulled her close to me.

'You are a clever woman, Roberta. That is why I...love you so much. Now listen, be rational. I have disappeared and walked through a door. A knife is pointless and so are your screams. If I was going to hurt you I would have done years ago. I have things to say to you. You would not let me say them before. Please let me say them now. Deal?' I said.

She stared at me as if looking at me for the first time. I tried to smile reassuringly at her but how could one be reassured in an event such as this?

At first she did nothing and kept staring at me. What a sight we must have made. Then she nodded her head.

'Do not scream when I release your mouth or so help me I will leave you to face what is coming and have nothing to do with it. If you want to be saved, be quiet, please.' I released her mouth and she let out a sigh.

'What the fuck is going on, Robert?' she asked. A reasonable question I am sure you would agree?

'Can we leave the bathroom and talk in the living room,' I suggested, getting out of the bath. I was expecting some resistance but she let me take her hand and help her out of the bath.

'I must say your idea of defending yourself is quite original. For future reference, if somebody genuinely wants to hurt you I would not go with that course of action.'

'I panicked.'

'Well of course you did. I disappeared in front of you. It is not the kind of thing you see every day. In fact, I think you were slightly underwhelmed,' I said.

We both found a seat. I smiled at her but she did not smile back. She was still confused and hurt. I had to be careful in my approach. Cockiness would not do in this matter. I must let her lead the way.

'You look awful,' she said.

'I guess I am a shade on the pale side.'

'So what you said before is true? You're not human?'

'No.'

'What are you?'

'To be honest, I do not know.'

'Some sort of demi-god?' she said. I laughed. She looked annoyed.

'No, no. I do not think so.' It seemed an inefficient reply but it was all that I had.

'I don't understand any of this. Why me?' she asked. It was coming to the part that I had dreaded.

'Why not?' I decided to say.

'Bullshit.'

'You are special,' I said. I looked at her with as much integrity and intensity as I could muster. I was so exhausted. The days were taking what was left of my life away from me. Every gesture was a mountain climbed. Every thought was an assault course.

'How?'

'You are what the world calls a Master.'

'A Master of what?'

'You are in the middle of creating a masterpiece,' I said.

'That crap that I'm writing? It's bargain bucket material,' she said. She reached for her cigarettes and took one out to light.

'Would you like one?' she said. I shook my head.

'Well I need one,' she decided. I watched her light the cigarette, her hand slightly shaking.

'It is not bargain bucket material. It is going to make 'Timelines for lines' seem like a children's book,' I said.

She scoffed at my words.

'You have got the wrong person and don't bring my mother into this.'

'She is already in it, Roberta.'

'What do you mean?'

'She is a Master too, well was,' I said. It pained me to say 'was' even more so now I had an emotional investment in her expiration as well as being the cause of it.

'So what? So what if she was and I am, according to you. I don't think that I am though.'

'No, I can see that. Trust me you are.'

'How do you know?'

'Because if you were not I would not have come for you. I would not have stalked you over the years and watched you grow up into the fine woman that you have become. Your mother would have been so proud of you. You are beautiful and talented like her.'

'Shut up,' she said. She still did not know how to take a compliment. Even her 'brush' with love with me had not enabled her to do this.

We sat in silence for a moment, digesting our exchanges, both not entirely sure of how the other felt regarding them.

'You have been following me for years you said?'

'Yes,' I said.

'What do you mean by your coming for me because I am a Master?' she asked. She placed her cigarette in the ashtray and folded her arms, awaiting my reply.

'This is the difficult part,' I said.
'As difficult as showing me that you can disappear or walk through walls?' she asked.
'Much harder.'
'Why have you come for me?' she said. She was not going to let me out of this one. This was a dance that had to be completed. She would say when the music could be stopped.

'What I am, whatever that is, has needs.'
'And?'
'These needs are not sexual. They are of the creative kind.'
'You've lost me. Needs of the creative kind? You have to paint or you will die kind?' she said. I was irritating her with my hesitation but she was also afraid. I could tell by the way that she folded her arms in a protective display.

'No, I must have painters or I will die but not just painters...any kind of creative person really.'
'You must have painters or you will die? I don't understand.'
'Do you ever wonder what drives you to write night after night while others are out drinking and partying?'
'Because I'm sad and pathetic,' she said.
'You know that is not the answer, Roberta. There is something within you that makes you want to write. You cannot describe it but it has always been there.

Since you were a child it has been there.'

I could see that she was listening to my words and relating to them. I decided to say nothing to allow her time to take in what I had said.

'I thought at first that I wanted to write because of my mother but as time went by I realised that I wanted to write for me, that I had to write,' she finally said.

'That is what makes a Master, the need to carry out their creative duties. A deep ache compels them to be who they are,' I said. I was talking like I knew every Master who had ever existed. This was, of course, not true, but I had known many and they were all born with the innate need to create.

'Why would you come for me? What can I give you?'
'Everything,' I said. She looked doubtful.
'What do you take? My work and claim it for your own? I don't understand what you could take from me.'

I did not want to answer the question for I knew what the aftermath of my words would be. I did not want to have to tell her the terrible truth of who I was and what I ate to survive but I could delay it no longer. I had come this far, I had to confess.

'I take your essence.'
'My essence?'
'Your essence is what makes you a Master. I do not know how I became what I did, this 'decadent' living off

the creative life force of others.' I hated myself for using the stranger's description of me but I had no other term to describe myself.

'How do you live of us?' she said. She had said 'us' which meant she had accepted that she was a Master all of a sudden. I was not sure if this was a good thing or not.

'Your essence is your pineal gland. That is your creative centre.'

'My pineal gland?'

'Yes, you see in Masters the gland does not calcify like it does in non-masters. When that gland calcifies all of the wonder that lives in the brain is lost. You have never lost your wonder.'

'But what are you saying? That you take the gland? Do you take the gland?' Her voice was showing traces of anxiety in it. Of course it would, the subject matter was unpleasant to say the least.

I could not find the words for an answer. I just nodded my head in response.

'You take glands? And what do you do with them?' she asked. I could not find the words.

'Robert, what do you do with the glands?' Still I could not find the words. I looked at her with an expression of resignation. This was the moment to end all moments with her. She would not want to know me after this. Is that why I was struck mute?

'You live of us? You live of our glands? Oh Jesus Christ. Do you eat our glands?' she said.

And still no words could come from me in that moment until she forced them out of me. She picked something up and threw it at me.

'Answer me,' she demanded.
'Yes,' I finally said.
'Yes what? I want to hear it.'
'I eat glands.'
'And you came for mine? You want to eat mine?'
'At first, yes,' I said.
'At first?'
'Yes, I have been watching you for so long. I thought I wanted you for your essence but somehow along the way something changed,' I said.

'What and now you don't want to eat my gland?' she said. I shook my head.
'What changed?' she said. I did not want to say the words that she wanted to hear. They were killing me slowly. I did not want to say them out loud.

'What changed, Robert?'
'My course of action changed. I no longer want your gland but somebody else does. That is why I am here, to warn you. Please do not complete the book. He will take you if you do. If you do not complete it you will be safe.'
'There are more of you?'

'Until recently I thought I was unique but another like

me now exists and he wants you. I beg of you not to complete the book.'

'I'm not going to promise that. This could be nonsense for all I know.'

'Nonsense? You can deceive yourself if you wish but your eyes cannot deceive you, Roberta. I am not human.'

She stared at me for some time. I could see her drinking in my features, now dull and pale, unlike the dashing, handsome man who she had first met.

'What happens if you don't eat an 'essence'?' she said. Her question suggested that she was starting to believe me or at least entertaining the idea.

'I do not know. I have never taken it that far. I always eat in the end but I cannot this time because you are the essence. I do not want to eat your essence.'

'Why not? You've eaten so many others. One more would not hurt,' she said. She was angry and fascinated all at once. I felt so tired. I knew what she wanted from me.

'Why have you exposed yourself like this? You should have let me complete and then taken me. Is that why you are so sick at the moment?' she asked. I nodded my head.

'Well let me make you better. I think I am a week away. You can have me when I complete. Help yourself.'

'I will not ever take you but he will. I beg you not to complete.'

'What do you do once you have taken the essence?

Can we live without it,' she asked.

'I do not know if you can or not. Some die naturally from the shock of it. Some I take the life of before that question can be answered.'

'How?' she said. Tears were starting to well in her eyes now. It pained me to watch her face, twisted with confusion and fear.

'I make it look like suicide,' I said. I noticed a tear start to fall from her eye.

'Would you have made me look like I had killed myself? Left my father to that fate? Knowing what happened to my mother?'

'No. Never. I have told you. At first I wanted your essence but then that 'want' changed into something else. I wanted you. I wanted you for you.'

She wiped her tears with the back of her hand. Her expression was changing. I could see that the pieces were falling into place for her.

'Please do not complete the book. He will come for you and I will not be able to stop him. I am too weak. You are so much more talented than your mother. That day I said all of those things, they were lies. I wanted you to stop writing because I knew what you were capable of,' I said.

I stood up and walked towards her.

'You did it,' she said. 'Stay back,' she added. I stood still, frozen in time. I knew what was going to happen next.

'You were there. I did see you. I did. I thought I recognised your face. You are shadow man,' she was whispering. She was staring straight ahead as if a projector was showing her pictures from her past and from that night in particular.

'I think I always knew you were, from the moment I saw you,' she said in an almost robotic tone.

'Please Roberta, let me-'

'- and I let you have me. You killed my mother and I let you have me.'

'Roberta, let me explain how I feel about you. The feelings that I have for you are real. I would rather die than take your essence from you.'

'You need to leave.'

'Please just let me-'

'-get out. Get out now. Get out of my house.' She was screaming at me. I started to back away from her. She was on me, pushing me towards the door.

'Get the fuck out of here, you murdering bastard.' The words were falling from her mouth as she opened the door.

'Please do not complete the novel. You will be safe if you do not complete.'

'Get out,' she said for a final time and pushed me into the hallway.

The door was slammed on me though it meant nothing. Had she not seen me walk through doors? I respected her need to put a barrier between us though.

I pressed my face against the wood. I could hear her crying, as silently as she could. I wanted to say to her that everything would be ok but I knew that she would not listen to my words any longer.

I waited for a short time, with my face pressed against the door. I felt the tears coming from my eyes. Is this what love is? Two people crying on different sides of a door? I hoped that she had listened to me and would not write. I was so weak I was not sure how long I could stay alive to guarantee her safety.

52. London - Present day

I had thought that by revealing the truth to Roberta that she would heed my warnings and place down the pen. My words just seemed to cause her even more anger and she was determined to finish her novel. She was either mad or did not believe what I had told her. She had seen me walk through walls and disappear. How much more evidence did she need for me to make her see?

As my body was closing down, due to my lack of essence eating, I knew what I had to do next. If she was determined to finish her novel then I would have to feed again to prevent her from being taken by the stranger. I did not want to do this but what other choice did I have? I could not take her and I would not stand back and watch the diabolical stranger feed on her.

There was the problem of a lack of Masters in this decade to contend with also. I had one other Master possibility. I knew that their essence would not be that strong but perhaps it would suffice to get me through this year and protect Roberta for as long as possible.

In some ways I wanted to just fade away. I prayed for a sudden end, for the decision to be made for me. This feeling did not last for long for not even I knew what happened in death. I did not know where my Masters went after my selfish acts. What if there was an afterlife and I had to endure it bearing witness to Roberta being consumed by the stranger?

I was afraid for myself also. What if all of my kills were waiting for me in 'eternity'? What if I had this all wrong and that despite my existence there was a God, as you mortals knew him. I could not handle my kills attacking me in a ghostly frame, tormenting me forever. I heard laughter and looked up in the direction where it was coming from.

'You truly are pathetic. You know as well as I do that there is no God or afterlife. There is only us. Our being in this room together is proof of that.'

'Get out of my room. Get out of my head,' I said. I sat

up. I could no longer lie down when he was in the room. He made me feel uneasy.

'Your kills would be so disappointed in your behaviour. What happened to the lothario who fucked and killed his way through the centuries?'

'You are disgusting,' I said.

'It is your life that I am relaying. Do not play the innocent with me. I have been watching you for a long time. Can you deny the flippant way that you have broken necks and drunk down your essences? You are the worst kind of junkie.'

'Fuck you,' I said and was immediately cross with myself. He smiled. I knew what he wanted to say but he spared me the response.

'Did you think any more on my offer? I think it is the best solution. It makes sense us teaming up. It will put paid to the loneliness that we both experience and we get half of her each. It will be a weak essence for the sharing but not as weak as the actor that you are thinking of feasting on. You could probably get a month from that essence if you are lucky.'

'I do not know what you are talking about,' I said.

He smiled again. He knew what I was talking about. Why could he read my thoughts so much better than I could his? I had not even been aware of his existence and yet he had been stalking me all of the time that I was stalking others.

'You can have him. You need him a lot more than I do. I am saving myself for Roberta. She is going to be amazing. When I rip her in two remember that I offered you a share.' He smiled and then he was gone before I could retaliate. What could I have said in response?

The actor in question had set the theatre world alight with his portrayals of various Shakespearean characters. Shakespeare was the man who had as much trouble with his identity as I did. Like me he has lived through the centuries, just not in physical form.

The actor had just finished for the evening his powerful projection (so said the critics) of Romeo. I had watched from the side lines and I did not feel that his performance matched up to the reviews but then I had been exposed to so many great actors through the centuries.

I was the spoilt child, exposed to too many toys and treats. I found it so hard to fall in love with today's creators for I had consumed so many of the trail blazers, the pioneers. Everything had become repetition to me. Still, he had beautiful eyes and a soothing voice. I had to latch on to the positives if I was to consume him and consume him I must.

He brushed past me as he exited the stage and I smelt the air around him. I could not sense a Master. I did not trust my senses. I hated the new me. I was so unsure of everything and everyone. It was like I had lost my sight and now I was being asked to read instructions before me without the guidance of Braille. I felt helpless.

Still, I followed him, in the way that only I could. I went unnoticed as I mimicked his steps to the dressing room. He was on his own, deep in thought. I had been following him for a few weeks, as best I could. I was so tired. Stalking was so much more draining for me than it used to be. He normally had company but tonight he was flying solo and so tonight would have to be the night for I was running out of time and this opportunity may not come again.

I watched as he sat at the dressing table. He stared at his reflection for a while before starting to remove his makeup. He stopped to light a cigarette. The clock in the corner was ticking away at me, demanding that I act before it was too late. The gentle tick was almost deafening as I tried to focus on the actor.

The procedure of removing the essence had been like second nature to me but now I felt sick to the pit of my stomach at the thought of consuming. I did not want this life any longer. Yes, as I stood in this room I decided there and then that my essence eating days were over. If it meant that I was over so be it.

I stepped behind him and watched him as he continued removing his theatre mask in between lugs on his cigarette. I stared at his neck and then at his eyes. It was the eyes, the eyes always killed me. I stared back at his neck. I felt revulsion. I had to consume to have the strength to fight the stranger for Roberta but I could not find the strength to go through with it.

'You coward,' a voice said. It was him. Before I could move or act, he swept in and removed the essence from the actor.

'I even gave you the chance to have him. You are an imbecile,' the stranger said. I looked at him and then at his hand. His hand held my salvation and yet I was rooted to the spot. If I could have killed myself then I think I would have.

The stranger looked at the essence and then back at me.

'It is no good,' he said before swallowing it. 'It is all but calcified,' he said with anger before smashing the dressing table mirror and taking a shard of glass and stabbing the actor through the neck.

'Shakespeare would approve,' he laughed. He put the shard into the actor's lifeless hand.

'Why?' I said. I stared at the actor's slumped body in the chair, a river of colour escaping from his neck.
'You said it was no good. Why kill him? Why consume?' I said.
'I consumed it to hide it. And kill? Why not? How many necks of the innocent have you broken just because?'

I could not respond. It had nothing to do with the fact that I was weak. I looked at my reflection in the cracked mirror. My image was distorted and broken just like my opinion of myself.

'You cannot protect yourself, let alone Roberta,' he said. He walked up to me and stroked my face with his bloody hand.

'The desperate times just got more desperate for you,' he said and licked my face.

'And for you too,' I managed to say.

'How so?'

'You said it yourself. Our only alternative to Roberta has an invalid essence. He was the second best chance of this year and he was no good. What will you do after you have consumed Roberta?'

I could not help but smile. My words unsettled him for I felt a weird kind of peace knowing that even if he won the battle he would never win the war for it would be the war to end all wars. An essence shortage meant that there was probably nothing but the end for us.

He did not speak as if to confirm what I thought. He was rattled. No emerging Masters had appeared in the past decade.

'We are a dying breed and just when I found you,' I said and smiled.

'I found you,' he said and left the room.

I had disturbed him and while I could feel myself

fading, this gave me some comfort. If I was to die at least I knew he would not be far behind me. Losing everything did not have to be a bad thing after all for the man who had nothing, had nothing to fear.

53. London - Present day (the final days)

As I write this Roberta is putting the finishing touches to her novel. She was always going to finish it. Think about it. Her mother was a feminist, an avid campaigner of independence. Would the daughter of Willow Downs let a man (for I was a man be it an unusual one) tell her what to do with her writing?

The last days were in some ways a relaxed affair though I could not get the images from the dressing room out of my mind. I had accepted our fates. Roberta would complete and I would try to defend her against the stranger and fail. She would die and I would die and our shared fate was enough for me.

If I am honest with myself, and I promised I would be from the start, I knew that she would be the reason I 'died' from the moment that I looked into her eyes. There is no greater emotion than seeing your life in the eyes of another. I had fought against it and pretended that I wanted her essence but it was never her essence that I craved. I had wanted her heart. I had become what I despised and I could live with it for I would not live for long.

'There would be no point in telling you not to complete anyway would there?' I whispered in her ear as she sat on the window ledge. She was looking at the rain falling outside. It always made her feel melancholy. It always reminded her of her mother.

'You came back,' she said, still looking at the rain.

'I never went,' I said. I managed to raise my hand to stroke her hair. She leant against my invisible fingers.

'Of course you did not,' she said and turned her head away from me again.

'And are you going to complete?' I said. I felt I had to ask the pointless question. She did not reply.

'I am not sorry that I called you a murdering coward,' she said instead. Her voice was not angry, it had warmth in it. This surprised me. I did not respond to it for she had nothing to feel sorry for. I was a murdering coward.

'Many men have hurt me in my time but I do believe that you have hurt me the most,' she said. She reached out to stroke the window. She ran her hand along the glass as if caressing a lover.

I winced at her words. What could I say to that? I had never wished to cause her such pain. The old me would have revelled in that sentence but who I found myself to be now?

'I can only say that I am sorry,' I said. It was a pathetic response but it was all I had in my reserve.

'And are you sorry that you killed my mother?' she asked.

'Lately, I am sorry every day. I am sorry every day,' I decided in that moment. She turned to look at me and found that I was not there. I had made myself invisible to her for I cut a pathetic figure. There were no physical traces of the man who she had fallen in love with.

'Are you still there?' she asked.

'Yes,' I said and placed my hand on her leg to confirm it.

'Are you dying?' she asked.

'We are all dying, Roberta,' I said.

'Stop being clever for once. Are you dying?'

'I think so.'

'Will my essence save you?' she asked.

'Yes, definitely,' I said. I squeezed her leg gently and let go off it.

'And yet you would ask that I not complete meaning death for you?' she said. She left the window sill and stood up.

'Show yourself to me,' she said.

'I cannot,' I said.

'I want to see you, please one more time,' she said.

After all that I had done to her could I deny her such a simple request? I materialised before her. The light in the room was dim but she could make out my features still. Her expression told me this. She held her hand against her mouth.

'I am beautiful am I not?' I said. I smiled but I could see she was on the verge of crying.

'Do not waste your tears on me. I am not worth it,' I said. She took me into her arms like I was a fragile ragdoll. I did not know how to feel as her warmth enveloped me. I could feel her beautiful heart beating against mine.

'You are worth it. Can you not understand why?' she asked through stifled sobs. I shook my head. I had taken her mother, destroyed her heart and her confidence. How was I worthy of her?

'You are willing to die for me. Do you understand now? There is no greater love than that,' she said. She pressed her lips to mine but I could not respond. I felt like I was choking, like all of the emotions that I had carried over the centuries had got stuck in my throat. Then there was nothing.

54. London - Present day

I awoke in Roberta's bed and the events of yesterday came racing back to me. She had held me and kissed my lips. Her actions had suggested that she had forgiven me. It was too much to hope for.

'You are awake,' she said. She entered the room and

had brought a coffee for me though I needed more than coffee for my weary body. I smiled all the same and managed to sit up. She handed the cup to me and sat on the edge of the bed.

'How do you feel?' she said. There were so many things I wished to say to her in response to that. I felt elation that she had forgiven me and terror at the unknown, of what was to come.

'I am ok,' I said. I sipped on the coffee. It was sweet. She still knew how I liked my drink. She had not forgotten.

'Can I ask you something?' she said.

'Anything,' I said. She lay down on the bed next to me on her side. She rested her head on her clutched fist.

'Will it hurt?'

'Will what hurt?'

'When he comes for my essence will I feel him taking it from me?' she said. It was a terrifying sentence to say and yet she said it with such composure.

'You will feel it, yes,' I said. I placed my cup down on the side.

'Will I die immediately or will I be alive when he makes it look like suicide?'

'I am not sure. I am not sure what he will do.'

'But you have done this so many times.'

'Yes but I am normally executing the procedure, not experiencing it. I am not sure what he will do.' This was a lie for I had seen the brutality that he had exhibited with the actor in the dressing room.

'But you must be able to tell by Masters' reactions if they are dead or alive.'
'I do not want to think about it,' I said.

I lay back down and stared at the vacuous white ceiling.

'You are feeling very weak aren't you?' she asked.
'Yes, I am,' I said. There was no point lying. It was obvious that I was not strong in my present condition.
'There is another way.'
'Do not say it.'
'I must. You could consume me.'
'I could not live with myself.'
'And you think that I can by letting you die like this when I have the cure?' she said, her tone annoyed.

'The cure is too much to ask for and it is only a temporary one. If there are no Masters after you I will die anyway and your life will be wasted for nothing.'

'I am going to be consumed by him, whoever he is. I would rather it be you. You will be gentle and ease me into my death. Will he ease me into death? I doubt it. Your choice leaves us both dead.'

'Choice? This is not a matter of choice, Roberta. If it was a matter of choice you would not complete and I would not have to worry about your safety. Then I could just see what my body does.'

'No, I have to complete,' she said and left the bed.
'You do not have to complete. She is not here to see it, Roberta. Nothing you do can bring her back.'

'This has nothing to do with my mother.'
'It has everything to do with her. You can lie to yourself but you cannot lie to me. I am an expert,' I said. How many lies had I told through the centuries to cover my reality?

My throat was dry. I let out a cough and struggled to lie on my side. Arguing was exhausting for me.

'I am finishing this book. It is up to you. You can either hold my hand as I edit the last word and take my essence or let him do his worst,' Roberta said.

She left the room. I stared into space. I had nothing left in me. I was not sure of anything.

55. California - 1935

I held the chloroform soaked cloth to her mouth and starting pressing it as hard as I could against her lips. She did not resist me. She was in fact, stroking my hand as I carried out the act. You see she was another Master who had suffered so much in life that death seemed like a day out at an amusement park. People who love life have a fear of death and then there were her kind.

When she became lifeless, I carried her to the

decorative sofa and placed her on it in the embryo position. She was, after all, reinventing herself, being born again through her own mortality. I stroked her hair and kissed her face which was still warm.

I stood up and stared at her, at my work. I was the Master of taking others and making it look like suicide. Sometimes it hurt to take a life but at times like this I felt nothing but pride and happiness. She had been diagnosed with breast cancer and so I had not killed her, I had taken her earlier than expected. She wanted this death. She did not want a painful, all absorbing terminal illness to ravish her. She wanted me.

Like all of my kills she had left at least one masterpiece for the world to remember her by. They would remember her work more than her death.

In some ways she had been a typical woman living in Victorian times and in other ways she was unique. She went from selling bars of soap door to door to cleaning up the male population's ideas of what it was to be a woman in her time. She wanted a better world, a truly progressive human race where capitalism was shunned and unity was the stitching that bound life's fabric together.

She had been on my Master radar for some time but in 1890 her mind unleashed so much poetry and prose that I had to come to her side. I had to soak in her radiating genius and warmth. I sat by her side as she created poetry, novellas and short stories. One short story in particular was the masterpiece that made me ache for her pineal gland. I watched her as she paced up and down the room and then leant against the wallpaper. Her eyes would widen at the decor and then her hand would stroke the walls and her mouth would crease.

I was actually in her presence when the idea formed for what is deemed to be her masterpiece. I did not stay to see it being completed but I was there when the spark lit up. There were other Masters to stalk and eat and so I left her to continue nurturing her ideas. I knew that I could have her whenever I wanted her.

She had been told to have minimum intellectual thoughts and not to touch a writing instrument for as long as she lived. She had obviously defied those 'medical' orders. There were times when she could not even feed or dress herself as she fought a 'brain disease'. In truth, she would have probably been diagnosed with post natal depression now but back then, this was not an option.

I have no idea why the memory of her has come to me now in these closing days. Perhaps because I recognise her defiance, in insisting that she write when she was told not to, in Roberta.

I do not know why my memories surface of past Masters like they choose to. Certain things trigger it for me with regards to her. If I see vivid wallpaper I walk over to it and run my hand along it just like she did all of those decades ago. As my hand runs along it I can smell the chloroform, I can hear her laboured breathing. My mind will not let me remember everything to protect me. It lets me see my past like a jigsaw puzzle with missing pieces.

I walk over to Roberta's wall and struggle to run my hand along it. There is no vivid wallpaper to be found. Just the magnolia surfaces of the 21st century. I yearn for a time when I could embrace flamboyance and when I could take the life of a female Master and justify it.

56. London - Present day

'Tonight,' Roberta said to the air of the living room. She knew I was hovering somewhere in the room, always at her side. I was a weakened but determined protector. I knew what she was telling me. She had gone to visit her father for the weekly dinner only this time it would be her last. Her father was not to know that. He would have held her tighter, or not even let her go, had he known it was the last time that he would see his daughter alive.

She had held his face just for a moment and kissed his head. She had told him that she loved him. These were the lasting images and words that she wanted her father to cling to when she was found dead. That would get him through the dark times. I had never known such grace and bravery before.

She picked up the photograph of the sea that her father had given to her, kissed it and placed it back down. She did the same with her parents' picture. She walked over to the book shelf and took down 'Timelines for lines' and ran her finger along the cover.

'I will live on through my work. We cannot live forever in any other way,' she said.

I watched as she poured a glass of wine and then sat at her computer. She opened up the book and went to the final editing spot.

'One sentence and it is finished. Where are you?' she asked me.

I materialised by her side. I could barely speak. She smiled. She sipped her wine. She placed the glass to my lips to offer me some. It trickled down the side of my mouth.

'It is time to celebrate. He is not here yet,' she said as she placed the glass down.

'He-will-come,' I managed to say.

'You will be ready,' she smiled and began to type. She looked at me for reassurance. I struggled to lift my arm to hover it near her neck.

'Do-not-want-to-do-this,' I managed to say. She took

my hand and stroked it.

'I want nothing more. You know what you must do when I finish this line.'

'Protect,' I whispered for the volume on my voice was turning down. How could I protect when I could not even speak?

'Eat,' she said. I grimaced.

She stared at the screen and for a moment longer and then she stopped typing. She smiled at me.

'It is done. I cannot improve on it,' she said.

I used every last bit of strength to get my hand to hover near her neck.

'I am done,' she said, a strength that I had never witnessed before in her voice. It made me love her even more.

We waited, my hand suspended in the air, her voice hanging in the air. I could feel my arm crying out to be lowered but I held it to her neck still. My limb shook violently.

The room became heavy with the threat of what was to come. My shaking arm sounded like an earthquake as I somehow held it in position. Where was the stranger? Why did he not come for his prize? I needed him to come. I was not sure how much longer I could keep my arm raised.

She smiled again at me. I tried to smile back. I wanted to let my arm fall to my side but I felt sure that the stranger was hiding, until I did just this, and then he would swoop in and claim her like he had claimed that poor actor.

'He is not coming?' Roberta asked me. She looked confused.
'I-cannot-say -for-certain' I managed to say.
'I love you,' she said.

The words weakened me all the more. After all I had done to her she still found it within her heart to say it. I could feel tears coming from my eyes again. I had lived through so many centuries and this was the only one that I had cried in the way that I did.

'Do not cry, be strong,' she said, though she cried herself. My arm was starting to lower. I could not hold it for much longer.

'You will have to take me, Robert,' she said. She pushed her neck against my arm. 'Take it, save yourself. I want to be with her. You have my blessing,' she insisted.

It was agony, indescribable agony. I shook my head as furiously as I could.

'Never,' I managed to say.

Then the air changed, it was as if the window had been

opened and a breeze was starting to invade the room. I knew what the change in temperature meant. He was here. He had come for her. I had seconds.

I looked into Roberta's eyes and she nodded her head. She looked so serene. I knew what she was saying to me without her speaking.

I somehow found it in me to begin the process that I was so familiar with and yet it felt so strange tonight. I felt what was left of my heart cracking as I started to pull her gland through her skin. It was agony for me.

When it was out, I had no time to stare at it like I often did. No time to think on the act that was about to take place. I swallowed it as quickly as I could and it almost got trapped in my throat for I was choking on the grief that my actions had just caused.

Roberta's head fell like a dead weight against me as the essence started to kick in to my system. I covered her mouth with my hand and started to smother her as gently as I could. I kept whispering that I loved her as my body started to stiffen. I held out for as long as I could until I knew that she had passed and then I allowed my body to fall to the floor.

At first I could hear screaming and then I realised that it was me. Then I was rendered speechless as the process took over my system and I saw the same images that I always had only this time everything was even more vivid. Was this because I had consumed both mother and daughter?

I positioned my body so I could not see Roberta's lifeless one. I stared at the ceiling. I could feel the stranger hovering by my side. I thought that I could hear laughter but I could not be sure of anything at present.

I thought that my mind would break with sorrow and yet I could also feel every part of my skin starting to rejuvenate in a way that I did not think was possible. She was saving me.

I was slowly coming alive again. Colour was rushing to my skin and my bones felt strong again. I could see clearly though my eyes were wet from tears.

With one final spasm I went into the intense orgasm that I always had when the essence had finally be consumed only this orgasm was marred with sadness that could not be measured. I wanted to be inside of Roberta and not her inside of me. I felt repulsed with myself.

I managed to pull myself up on to my knees and I vomited violently. Then I saw her. Her body slumped in the chair still, as if she had fallen asleep in an awkward fashion. How I wished that to be the truth.

I started to crawl towards her. I heard clapping. It was coming from the stranger. I ignored it.

'You are back,' he said as I pulled Roberta up from the

chair and carried her lifeless frame to the couch. I thought that my knees would give out but I remained upright.

I lay her down and put a cushion under her head. Her face looked surprisingly peaceful. I kissed her lips and then fell on to her chest. I cried the cry of centuries of killing, accumulating in the taking of one who I had loved. I cannot describe the noises that came from me. They were primal, sublime. I cried until there was nothing left. I fell against the couch, managing to rest my back against it.

I looked for the stranger. He was standing near me with a strange expression on his face.

'Now the real story begins, my friend,' he said with that confident smile that I so despised.

I was lost in that moment but I was also found.

A Note From The Author.

While writing 'The Decadent' I started to think about the probability of there being a Decadent in reality. So many creative Masters have died in weird circumstances and this is what actually inspired me to write this work of fiction.

What if this debut novel of mine is a masterpiece? Will the Decadent come out of the shadows and claim me like he has claimed so many others, including the love of his life?

There is so much more to come but I must write in stages. As long as I write this story in instalments he cannot come for me. I am sorry if this is an inconvenience for you but would it not be more inconvenient of me to finish the story and allow him to take me when there is so much more to tell?

Printed in Great Britain
by Amazon